The Skipper's Wooing by W.W. Jacobs
& THE BROWN MAN'S SERVANT

William Wymark Jacobs was born on September 8th, 1863 in the Wapping district of London, England. Jacobs grew up near the docks, where his father was a wharf manager. The docks and river side would be a constant theme of his writing in years to come.

Although surrounded by poverty, he received a formal education in London, first at a private prep school and later at the Birkbeck Literary and Scientific Institute.

His working life began with a less than exciting clerical position at the Post Office Savings Bank. Jacobs put his imagination to good use writing short stories, sketches and articles, many for the Post Office house publication "Blackfriars Magazine."

In 1896 Jacobs published Many Cargoes, a selection of sea-faring yarns, which established him as a popular writer with a knack for authentic dialogue and trick endings.

A year later he published a novelette, The Skipper's Wooing, and in 1898 another collection of short stories; Sea Urchins. These works painted vivid pictures of dockland and seafaring London full of colourful characters.

By 1899, Jacobs was able to quit the post office and write full-time.

He married the noted suffragist Agnes Eleanor Williams (who had been jailed for her protest activities) in 1900. They set up households both in Loughton, Essex and in central London.

The publication in 1902 of At Sunwich Port and Dialstone Lane, in 1904, cemented Jacobs' reputation as one of the leading British authors of the new century.

There followed a string of further successful publications, including Captain's All (1905), Night Watches (1914), The Castaways (1916), and Sea Whispers (1926).

Though Jacobs would create little in the way of new work after 1911, he still wrote and was recognized as a leading humorist, ranked alongside such writers as P. G. Wodehouse.

William Wymark Jacobs died in a North London nursing home in Hornsey Lane, Islington on September 1st, 1943.

Index of Contents

CHAPTER I

The schooner Seamew, of London, Captain Wilson master and owner, had just finished loading at Northfleet with cement for Brittlesea. Every inch of space was packed. Cement, exuded from the cracks, imparted to the hairy faces of honest seamen a ghastly appearance sadly out of keeping with their characters, and even took its place, disguised as thickening, among the multiple ingredients of a sea-pie that was cooking for dinner.

It was not until the decks were washed and the little schooner was once more presentable that the mate gave a thought to his own toilet. It was a fine, warm morning in May, and some of the cargo had got into his hair and settled in streaks on his hot, good-humored face. The boy had brought aft a wooden bucket filled with fair water, and placed upon the hatch by its side a piece of yellow soap and a towel. Upon these preparations the mate smiled pleasantly, and throwing off his shirt and girding his loins with his braces, he bent over and with much zestful splashing began his ablutions.

Twice did the ministering angel, who was not of an age to be in any great concern about his own toilet, change the water before the mate was satisfied; after which the latter, his face and neck aglow with friction, descended to the cabin for a change of raiment.

He did not appear on deck again until after dinner, which, in the absence of the skipper, he ate alone. The men, who had also dined, were lounging forward, smoking, and the mate, having filled his own pipe, sat down by himself and smoked in silence.

"I'm keeping the skipper's dinner 'ot in a small sorsepan, sir," said the cook, thrusting his head out of the galley.

"All right," said the mate.

"It's a funny thing where the skipper gets to these times," said the cook, addressing nobody in particular, but regarding the mate out of the corner of his eye.

"Very rum," said the mate, who was affably inclined just then.

The cook came out of the galley, and, wiping his wet hands on his dirty canvas trousers, drew near and gazed in a troubled fashion ashore.

"'E's the best cap'n I ever sailed under," he said slowly. "Ain't it struck you, sir, he's been worried like these 'ere last few trips? I told 'im as 'e was goin' ashore as there was sea-pie for dinner, and 'e ses, 'All right, Joe' 'e ses, just as if I'd said boiled beef and taters, or fine mornin', sir, or anythink like that!"

The mate shook his head, blew out a cloud of smoke and watched it lazily as it disappeared.

"It strikes me as 'ow 'e'sarter fresh cargo or something," said a stout old seaman who had joined the cook. "Look 'ow 'e's dressing nowadays! Why, the cap'n of a steamer ain't smarter!"

"Not so smart, Sam," said the remaining seaman, who, encouraged by the peaceful aspect of the mate had also drawn near. "I don't think it's cargo he's after, though—cement pays all right."

"It ain't cargo," said a small but confident voice.

"You clear out!" said old Sam. "A boy o' your age shovin' his spoke in when 'is elders is talkin'! What next, I wonder!"

"Where am I to clear to? I'm my own end of the ship anyway," said the youth vindictively.

The men started to move, but it was too late. The mate's latent sense of discipline was roused and he jumped up in a fury.

"My!" he said, "if there ain't the whole blasted ship's company aft—every man Jack of 'em! Come down in the cabin, gentlemen, come down and have a drop of Hollands and a cigar apiece. All the riffraff o' the foc'sle sitting aft and prattling about the skipper like a parcel o' washerwomen. And smoking, by—! smoking! Well, when the skipper comes aboard he'll have to get a fresh crew or a fresh mate. I'm sick of it. Why, it might be a barge for all the discipline that's kept! The boy's the only sailor among you."

He strode furiously up and down the deck; the cook disappeared into the galley, and the two seamen began to bustle about forward. The small expert who had raised the storm, by no means desirous of being caught in the tail of it, put his pipe in his pocket and looked round for a job.

"Come here!" said the mate sternly.

The boy came towards him.

"What was that you were saying about the skipper?" demanded the other.

"I said it wasn't cargo he was after," said Henry.

"Oh, a lot you know about it!" said the mate.

Henry scratched his leg, but said nothing.

"A lot you know about it!" repeated the mate in rather a disappointed tone.

Henry scratched the other leg.

"Don't let me hear you talking about your superior officer's affairs again," said the mate sharply. "Mind that!"

"No, sir," said the boy humbly. "It ain't my business, o; course."

"What isn't your business?" said the mate carelessly. "His," said Henry.

The mate turned away seething, and hearing a chuckle from the galley, went over there and stared at the cook—a wretched being with no control at all over his feelings—for quite five minutes. In that short space of time he discovered that the galley was the dirtiest hole under the sun and the cook the uncleanest person that ever handled food. He imparted his discoveries to the cook, and after reducing him to a state of perspiring imbecility, turned round and rated the men again. Having charged them with insolence when they replied, and with sulkiness when they kept silent, he went below, having secured a complete victory, and the incensed seamen, after making sure that he had no intention of returning, went towards Henry to find fault with him.

"If you was my boy," said Sam, breathing heavily, "I'd thrash you to within a inch of your life."

"If I was your boy I should drown myself," said Henry very positively.

Henry's father had frequently had occasion to remark that his son favored his mother, and his mother possessed a tongue which was famed throughout Wapping, and obtained honorable mention in distant Limehouse.

"You can't expect discipline aboard a ship where the skipper won't let you 'it the boy," said Dick moodily. "It's bad for 'im too."

"Don't you worry about me, my lads," said Henry with offensive patronage. "I can take care of myself all right. You ain't seen me come aboard so drunk that I've tried to get down the foc'sle without shoving the scuttle back. You never knew me to buy a bundle o' forged pawn-tickets. You never—"

"Listen to 'im," said Sam, growing purple; "I'll be 'ung for 'im yet."

"If you ain't, I will," growled Dick, with whom the matter of the pawn-tickets was a sore subject.

"Boy!" yelled the mate, thrusting his head out at the companion.

"Coming, sir!" said Henry. "Sorry I can't stop any longer," he said politely; "but me an' the mate's going to have a little chat."

"I'll have to get another ship," said Dick, watching the small spindly figure as it backed down the companion-ladder. "I never was on a ship afore where the boy could do as he liked."

Sam shook his head and sighed. "It's the best ship I was ever on, barrin' that," he said sternly.

"What'll 'e be like when he grows up?" demanded Dick, as he lost himself in the immensity of the conjecture. "It ain't right t' the boy to let him go on like that. One good hidin' a week would do 'im good and us too."

Meantime the object of their care had reached the cabin, and, leaning against the fireplace, awaited the mate's pleasure.

"Where's the cap'n?" demanded the latter, plunging at once into the subject.

Henry turned and looked at the small clock.

"Walkin' up and down a street in Gravesend," he said deliberately.

"Oh, you've got the second-sight, I s'pose," said the mate reddening. "And what's he doing that for?"

"To see 'er come out," said the boy.

The mate restrained himself, but with difficulty.

"And what'll he do when she does come out?" he demanded.

"Nothin'," replied the seer with conviction. "What are you lookin' for?" he inquired, with a trace of anxiety in his voice, as the mate rose from the locker, and, raising the lid, began groping for something in the depths.

"Bit o' rope," was the reply.

"Well, what did yer ask me for?" said Henry with hasty tearfulness. "It's the truth. 'E won't do nothin'; 'e never does—only stares."

"D'you mean to say you ain't been gammoning me?" demanded the mate, seizing him by the collar.

"Come and see for yourself," said Henry.

The mate released him, and stood eyeing him with a puzzled expression as a thousand-and-one little eccentricities on the part of the skipper suddenly occurred to him.

"Go and make yourself tidy," he said sharply; "and mind if I find you've been doing me I'll flay you alive."

The boy needed no second bidding. He dashed up on deck and, heedless of the gibes of the crew, began a toilet such as he had never before been known to make within the memory of man.

"What's up, kiddy?" inquired the cook, whose curiosity became unbearable.

"Wot d'you mean?" demanded Henry with dignity.

"Washin', and all that," said the cook, who was a plain creature.

"Don't you ever wash yourself, you dirty pig?" said Henry elegantly. "I s'pose you think doin' the cookin' keeps you clean, though."

The cook wrung his hands, and, unconscious of plagiarism, told Sam he'd be 'ung for 'im.

"Me and the mate are goin' for a little stroll, Sam," observed the youth as he struggled into his jersey. "Keep your eyes open, and don't get into mischief. You can give Slushy a 'and with the sorsepans if you've got nothin' better to do. Don't stand about idle."

The appearance of the mate impeded Sam's utterance, and he stood silently by the others, watching the couple as they clambered ashore. It was noticed that Henry carried his head very erect, but whether this was due to the company he was keeping or the spick-and-span appearance he made, they were unable to determine.

"Easy—go easy," panted the mate, mopping his red face with a handkerchief. "What are you in such a hurry for?"

"We shall be too late if we don't hurry," said Henry; "then you'll think I've been tellin' lies."

The mate made no further protest, and at the same rapid pace they walked on until they reached a quiet road on the outskirts of Gravesend.

"There he is!" said Henry triumphantly, as he stopped and pointed up the road at the figure of a man slowly pacing up and down. "She's at a little school up at the other end. A teacher or somethin'. Here they come."

As he spoke a small damsel with a satchel and a roll of music issued from a house at the other end of the road, the advanced guard of a small company which in twos and threes now swarmed out and went their various ways.

"Nice girls, some of 'em!" said Henry, glancing approvingly at them as they passed. "Oh, here she comes! I can't say I see much in her myself."

The mate looked up and regarded the girl as she approached with considerable interest. He saw a pretty girl with nice gray eyes and a flush, which might be due to the master of the Seamew—who was following at a respectful distance behind her—trying to look unconcerned at this unexpected appearance.

"Halloa, Jack!" he said carelessly.

"Halloa!" said the mate, with a great attempt at surprise. "Who'd ha' thought o' seeing you here!"

The skipper, disdaining to reply to this hypocrisy, stared at Henry until an intelligent and friendly grin faded slowly from that youth's face and left it expressionless. "I've just been having a quiet stroll," he said, slowly turning to the mate.

"Well, so long!" said the latter, anxious to escape.

The other nodded, and turned to resume his quiet stroll at a pace which made the mate hot to look at him. "He'll have to look sharp if he's going to catch her now," he said thoughtfully.

"He won't catch her," said Henry; "he never does—leastways if he does he only passes and looks at her out of the corner of his eye. He writes letters to her of a night, but he never gives 'em to her."

"How do you know?" demanded the other.

"Cos I look at 'im over his shoulder while I'm puttin' things in the cupboard," said Henry.

The mate stopped and regarded his hopeful young friend fixedly.

"I s'pose you look over my shoulder too, sometimes?" he suggested.

"You never write to anybody except your wife," said Henry carelessly, "or your mother. Leastways I've never known you to."

"You'll come to a bad end, my lad," said the mate thickly; "that's what you'll do."

"What 'e does with 'em I can't think," continued Henry, disregarding his future. "'E don't give 'em to 'er. Ain't got the pluck, I s'pose. Phew! Ain't it 'ot!"

They had got down to the river again, and he hesitated in front of a small beer-shop whose half open door and sanded floor offered a standing invitation to passers-by.

"Could you do a bottle o' ginger-beer?" inquired the mate, attracted in his turn.

"No," said Henry shortly, "I couldn't. I don't mind having what you're going to have."

The mate grinned, and, leading the way in, ordered refreshment for two, exchanging a pleasant wink with the proprietor as that humorist drew the lad's half-pint in a quart pot.

"Ain't you goin' to blow the head off, sir?" inquired the landlord as Henry, after glancing darkly into the depths and nodding to the mate, buried his small face in the pewter. "You'll get your moustache all mussed up if you don't."

The boy withdrew his face, and, wiping his mouth with the back of his hand, regarded the offender closely. "So long as it don't turn it red I don't mind," he said patiently, "and I don't think as 'ow your swipes would hurt anythin'."

He went out, followed by the mate, leaving the landlord wiping down the counter with one hand while he mechanically stroked his moustache with the other. By the time a suitable retort occurred to him the couple were out of earshot.

CHAPTER II

Captain Wilson, hot with the combined effects of exercise and wrath, continued the pursuit, but the pause to say sweet nothings to the second in command was fatal to his success. He had often before had occasion to comment ruefully upon the pace of the quarry, and especially at such times when he felt that he had strung his courage almost up to speaking point. To-day he was just in time to see her vanish into the front garden of a small house, upon the door of which she knocked with expressive vigor. She disappeared into the house just as he reached the gate.

"Damn the mate!" he said irritably—"and the boy," he added, anxious to be strictly impartial.

He walked on aimlessly at a slow pace until the houses ended and the road became a lane shaded with tall trees and flanked by hawthorn hedges. Along this he walked a little way, and then, nervously fingering a note in his jacket pocket, retraced his steps.

"I'll see her and speak to her anyway," he muttered. "Here goes."

He walked slowly back to the house, and, with his heart thumping, and a choking sensation in his throat, walked up to the door and gave a little whisper of a knock upon it. It was so faint that, after waiting a considerable time, he concluded that it had not been heard, and raised the knocker again. Then the door opened suddenly, and the knocker, half detained in his grasp, slipped from his fingers and fell with a crash that made him tremble at his hardihood. An elderly woman with white hair opened the door. She repressed a start and looked at him inquiringly.

"Cap'n Jackson in?" inquired the skipper, his nerves thoroughly upset by the knocker.

"Who?" said the other.

"Cap'n Jackson," repeated the skipper, reddening.

"There is no such man here," said the old woman. "Are you sure it is Captain Jackson you want?" she added.

"I'm—I'm not sure," said Wilson truthfully.

The old woman looked at him eagerly. "Will you come in?" she said slowly, and, without giving him time to refuse, led the way into the small front room. The skipper followed her with the conscience of a fox invited into a poultry yard, and bringing up in the doorway, gazed uncomfortably at the girl who had risen at his entrance.

"This gentleman is inquiring for a Captain Jackson," said the old woman, turning to the girl. "I thought he—he doesn't seem quite sure whether it is Captain Jackson he wants—he may bring news," she concluded incoherently.

"It's not likely, mother," said the girl, regarding the adventurous mariner by no means favorably. "There is no Captain Jackson here, sir."

"Have you been looking for him long?" inquired the mother.

"Years and years," said the other, forgetting himself.

The old woman sighed sympathetically. "Won't you sit down?" she said.

"Thank you," said the skipper, and took the edge of the sofa.

"You're not quite certain of the name?" suggested the girl coldly.

"It—it sounded like Jackson," murmured the intruder in a small, modest voice. "It might have been Blackson, or Dackson, or even Snackson—I won't swear to it."

The old woman put her hand to her brow. "I thought perhaps you might have brought me some news of my poor husband," she said at length. "I lost him some years ago, and when you came here inquiring for a seafaring man I thought you might somehow have brought news."

"You must see, mother, that this gentleman is looking for somebody else," said the girl; "you are hindering him from finding Captain Jackson."

"If he's been looking for him for years," said the old woman, bridling mildly, "a few minutes will not make much difference."

"Certainly not," said Wilson, in a voice which he tried in vain to make stronger. "When you say lost, ma'am, you mean missing?"

"Five years," said the old woman, shaking her head and folding her hands in her lap. "How long do you say you've been looking for Captain Jackson?"

"Seven," said the skipper with a calmness which surprised himself.

"And you haven't given up hope, I suppose?"

"Not while life lasts," said the other, studying the carpet.

"That's the way I feel," said the old woman energetically. "What a surprise it'll be when you meet him!"

"For both of them," said the girl.

"It's five years last May—the 20th of May," said the old woman, "since I last saw my poor husband. He—"

"It can't be of any interest to this gentleman, mother," interposed the girl.

"I'm very much interested, ma'am," said the skipper defiantly; "besides, when I'm looking for poor Jackson, who knows I mightn't run up against the other."

"Ah! who knows but what you might," said the old woman. "There's one gentleman looking for him now—Mr. Glover, my daughter's husband that is to be."

There was a long pause, then the skipper, by dint of combining his entire stock of Christianity and politeness, found speech. "I hope he finds him," he said slowly.

"All that a man can do he's doing," said the old lady. "He's a commercial traveller by trade, and he gets about a great deal in the way of business."

"Have you tried advertising?" inquired the skipper, striving manfully to keep his interest up to its former pitch.

The other shook her head and looked uneasily at her daughter.

"It wouldn't be any good," she said in a low voice—"it wouldn't be any good."

"Well, I don't want to pry into your business in any way," said Wilson, "but I go into a good many ports in the course of the year, and if you think it would be any use my looking about I'll be pleased and proud to do so, if you'll give me some idea of who to look for."

The old lady fidgeted with all the manner of one half desiring and half fearing to divulge a secret.

"You see we lost him in rather peculiar circumstances," she said, glancing uneasily at her daughter again. "He—"

"I don't want to know anything about that, you know, ma'am," interposed the skipper gently.

"It would be no good advertising for my father," said the girl in her clear voice, "because he can neither read nor write. He is a very passionate, hasty man, and five years ago he struck a man down and thought he had killed him. We have seen nothing and heard nothing of him since."

"He must have been a strong man," commented the skipper.

"He had something in his hand," said the girl, bending low over her work. "But he didn't hurt him really. The man was at work two days after, and he bears him no ill-will at all."

"He might be anywhere," said the skipper, meditating.

"He would be sure to be where there are ships," said the old lady; "I'm certain of it. You see he was captain of a ship himself a good many years, and for one thing he couldn't live away from the water, and for another it's the only way he has of getting a living, poor man—unless he's gone to sea again, which isn't likely."

"Coasting trade, I suppose?" said the skipper, glancing at two or three small craft which were floating in oil round the walls.

The old lady nodded. "Those were his ships," she said, following his glance; "but the painters never could get the clouds to please him. I shouldn't think there was a man in all England harder to please with clouds than he was."

"What sort of looking man is he?" inquired Wilson.

"I'll get you a portrait," said the old lady, and she rose and left the room.

The girl from her seat in the window by the geraniums stitched on steadily. The skipper, anxious to appear at his ease, coughed gently three times, and was on the very verge of a remark—about the weather—when she turned her head and became absorbed in something outside. The skipper fell to regarding the clouds again with even more disfavor than the missing captain himself could have shown.

"That was taken just before he disappeared," said the old lady, entering the room again and handing him a photograph. "You can keep that."

The skipper took it and gazed intently at the likeness of a sturdy full-bearded man of about sixty. Then he placed it carefully in his breast-pocket and rose to his feet.

"And if I should happen to drop across him," he said slowly, "what might his name be?"

"Gething," said the old lady, "Captain Gething. If you should see him, and would tell him that he has nothing to fear, and that his wife and his daughter Annis are dying to see him, you will have done what I can never, never properly thank you for."

"I'll do my best," said the other warmly. "Good-afternoon."

He shook hands with the old woman, and then, standing with his hands by his side, looked doubtfully at Annis.

"Good-afternoon," she said cheerfully.

Mrs. Gething showed him to the door.

"Any time you are at Gravesend, captain, we shall be pleased to see you and hear how you get on," she said as she let him out.

The captain thanked her, pausing at the gate to glance covertly at the window; but the girl was bending over her work again, and he walked away rapidly.

Until he had reached his ship and was sitting down to his belated dinner he had almost forgotten, in the joyful excitement of having something to do for Miss Gething, the fact that she was engaged to another man. As he remembered this he pushed his plate from him, and, leaning his head on his hand, gave way to a fit of deep melancholy. He took the photograph from his pocket, and, gazing at it intently, tried to discover a likeness between the father and daughter. There was not sufficient to warrant him in bestowing a chaste salute upon it.

"What do you think o' that?" he inquired, handing it over to the mate, who had been watching him curiously.

"Any friend o' yours?" inquired the mate, cautiously.

"No," said the other.

"Well, I don't think much of him," said the mate. "Where d'you get it?"

"It was given to me," said the skipper. "He's missing, and I've got to find him if I can. You might as well keep your eyes open too."

"Where are you going to look for him?" asked the mate.

"Everywhere," said the other. "I'm told that he's likely to be in a seaport town, and if you'll be on the look-out I'll take it as a favor."

"I'll do that, o' course," said the mate. "What's he been doing?"

"Nothing that I know of," said the skipper; "but he's been missing some five years, and I promised I'd do my best to find him."

"Friends are anxious, I s'pose?" said the mate.

"Yes," said the other.

"I always find," continued the mate, "that women are more anxious in these sort o' cases than men."

"More tender-hearted," said the skipper.

"It ain't a bad sort o' face, now I come to look at it," said the baffled mate, regarding it closely. "Seems to me I've seen somebody very much like it—a girl, I think—but I can't say where."

"Bearded lady at a fair, I should think," said the skipper bluffly.

Conversation was interrupted by the appearance of Henry, who, seeing the photograph in the mate's hand, at once began putting the butter away. A glance told him that the mate was holding it upside down, and conscience told him that this was for his benefit. He therefore rigidly averted his gaze while clearing the table, and in a small mental ledger, which he kept with scrupulous care for items such as these, made a debit entry in the mate's account.

"Boy," said the skipper suddenly.

"Sir," said Henry.

"You're a fairly sharp youngster, I think," said the skipper. "Take hold o' that photo there."

Henry's face suffused with a great joy. He looked derisively at the mate and took the photograph from him, listening intently to much the same instructions as had been previously given to the mate. "And you can take it for'ard," concluded the skipper, "and let the men see it."

"The men?" said Henry in astonishment.

"Yes, the men; don't I speak plain?" retorted the skipper.

"Very plain, sir," said the boy; "but they'll only make a muddle of it, sir. Fancy fat Sam and the cook and Dick!"

"Do as you're told!" said the other irascibly.

"O' course, sir," said Henry, "but they'll only worry me with a lot o' questions as to who 'e is an' wot you want 'im for."

"You take it for'ard," said the skipper, "and tell them there's a couple of sovereigns for the first man that finds him."

The youth took the photograph, and after another careful scrutiny, with the object of getting a start in the race for wealth, took it forward. Fat Sam, it seemed, had seen the very man only two days before at Poplar; the cook knew his features as well as he knew those of his own mother, while Dick had known him for years as an old and respected inhabitant of Plymouth. Henry went back to the skipper, and, having furnished him with this information, meekly suggested that they should drag Gravesend first.

It was midnight when they got the anchor up and dropped silently down the river. Gravesend was silent, and the dotted lines of street lamps shone over a sleeping town as the Seamew crept softly by.

A big steamer in front whistled warningly for the pilot's boat, and slowing up as the small craft shot out from the shore to meet it, caused a timely diversion to the skipper's melancholy by lying across his bows. By the time he had fully recovered from the outrage and had drunk a cup of coffee, which had been prepared in the galley, Gravesend had disappeared round the bend, and his voluntary search had commenced.

CHAPTER III

They made Brittlesea in four days—days in which the skipper, a prey to gentle melancholy, left things mostly to the mate. Whereupon melancholia became contagious, and Sam's concertina having been impounded by the energetic mate, disaffection reared its ugly head in the foc'sle and called him improper names when he was out of earshot.

They entered the small river on which stands the ancient town of Brittlesea at nightfall. Business for the day was over. A few fishermen, pipe in mouth, lounged upon the quay, while sounds of revelry, which in some mysterious way reminded the crew of their mission to find Captain Gething, proceeded from the open doors of a small tavern opposite. The most sanguine of them hardly expected to find him the first time; but, as Sam said, the sooner they started the better. For all they knew he might be sitting in that very public-house waiting to be found.

They went ashore a little later and looked for him there, but without success. All they did find was a rather hot-tempered old man, who, irritated by the searching scrutiny of the cook, asked him shortly whether he had lost anything, because, if so, and he, the cook, thought he was sitting on it, perhaps he'd be good enough to say so. The cook having replied in fitting terms, they moved off down the quay to the next tavern. Here they fared no better, Dick declaring that the beer was if anything worse than the other, and that nobody who had lived in the place any time would spend his money there. They therefore moved on once more, and closing time came before their labors were half completed.

"It's quite a little romans," said Sam thickly, as he was pushed outside the last house of call, and a bolt shot desolately behind him. "Where shall we go now?"

"Get back to the ship," said Dick; "come along."

"Not 'fore I foun' 'im," said Sam solemnly, as he drew back from Dick's detaining hand.

"You won't find him to-night, Sam," said the cook humorsomely.

"Why not?" said Sam, regarding him with glassy eyes. "We came out fin' 'im!"

"Cos it's dark, for one thing," said the cook.

Sam laughed scornfully.

"Come on!" said Dick, catching him by the arm again.

"I come out fin' cap'n, cap'n—fin' 'im," said Sam. "I'm not goin' back 'thout 'im."

He rolled off down the road, and the two men, the simple traditions of whose lives forbade them to leave a shipmate when in that condition, followed him, growling. For half an hour they walked with him through the silent streets of the little town. Dick with difficulty repressing his impatience as the stout seaman bent down at intervals and thoroughly searched doorsteps and other likely places for the missing man. Finally, he stopped in front of a small house, walked on a little way, came back, and then, as though he had suddenly made up his mind, walked towards it.

"Hold him, cook!" shouted Dick, throwing his arms around him.

The cook flung his arms round Sam's neck, and the two men, panting fiercely, dragged him away.

"Now you come aboard, you old fool!" said Dick, losing his temper; "we've had enough o' your games."

"Leg go!" said Sam, struggling.

"You leave that knocker alone, then," said Dick warningly.

"'E's in there!" said Sam, nodding wisely at the house.

"You come back, you old fool!" repeated Dick. "You never 'ort to 'ave nothin' stronger than milk."

"Ole my coat, cookie!" said Sam, his manner changing suddenly to an alarming sternness.

"Don't be a fool, Sam!" said the cook entreatingly.

"'Ole my coat!" repeated Sam, eyeing him haughtily.

"You know you haven't got a coat on," said the cook appealingly. "Can't you see it's a jersey? You ain't so far gone as all that!"

"Well, 'ole me while I take it off," said Sam, sensibly.

Against his better sense the cook steadied the stout seaman while he proceeded to peel, Dick waited until the garment—a very tight one—was over his head, and then, pushing the cook aside, took his victim and made him slowly gyrate on the pavement.

"Turn round three times and catch who you can, Sam," he said cruelly. "Well, sit down, then."

He lowered him to the pavement, and, accompanied by the cook, drew off and left him to his fate. Their last glance showed them a stout, able-bodied seaman, with his head and arms confined in a jersey, going through contortions of an extraordinary nature to free himself, and indulging in language which, even when filtered by the garment in question, was of a singularly comprehensive and powerful description. He freed himself at last, and after flinging the garment away in his anger, picked it up again, and, carrying it under his arm, zigzagged his way back to the ship.

His memory when he awoke next morning was not quite clear, but a hazy recollection of having been insulted led him to treat Dick and the cook with marked coldness, which did not wear off until they were all busy on deck. Working at cement is a dry job, and, after hardening his heart for some time, the stout seaman allowed the cook to call him to the galley and present him with a mug of cold coffee left from the cabin table.

The cook washed the mug up, and, preferring the dusty deck to the heat of the fire, sat down to wash a bowl of potatoes. It was a task which lent itself to meditation, and his thoughts, as he looked wistfully at the shore, reverted to Captain Gething and the best means of finding him. It was clear that the photograph was an important factor in the search, and, possessed with a new idea, he left the potatoes and went down to the cabin in search of it. He found it on a shelf in the skipper's state-room, and, passing up on deck again, stepped ashore.

From the first three people he spoke to he obtained no information whatever. They all inspected the photograph curiously and indulged in comments, mostly unfavorable, but all agreed that there was nobody like it in Brittlesea. He had almost given it up as a bad job, and was about to return, when he saw an aged fisherman reclining against a post.

"Fine day, mate," said the cook.

The old man courteously removed a short clay pipe from his puckered mouth in order to nod, and replacing it, resumed his glance seaward.

"Ever seen anybody like that?" inquired the cook, producing the portrait.

The old man patiently removed the pipe again, and taking the portrait, scanned it narrowly.

"It's wonderful how they get these things up nowadays," he said in a quavering voice; "there was nothing like that when you an' me was boys."

"There 'as been improvements," admitted the cook indignantly.

"All oils they was," continued the old man meditatively, "or crains."

"'Ave you ever seen anybody like that?" demanded the cook impatiently.

"Why, o' course I have. I'm goin' to tell you in a minute," said the old man querulously. "Let me see— what's his name again?"

"I don't know 'is name," said the cook untruth-fully.

"I should know it if I was to hear it," said the old man slowly. "Ah, I've got it! I've got it!"

He tapped his head triumphantly, and, with a bleared, shining old eye, winked at the cook.

"My memory's as good as ever it was," he said complacently. "Sometimes I forget things, but they come back. My mother used to be the same, and she lived to ninety-three."

"Lor!" interrupted the anxious cook. "What's the name?"

The old man stopped. "Drat it!" he said, with a worried look, "I've lost it again; but it'll come back."

The cook waited ten minutes for the prodigal. "It ain't Gething, I s'pose?" he said at length.

"No," said the old man; "don't you be in a hurry; it'll come back."

"When?" asked the cook rebelliously.

"It might be in five minutes' time, and it might be in a month," said the old man firmly, "but it'll come back."

He took the portrait from the hands of the now sulky cook and strove to jog his memory with it.

"John Dunn's his name," he cried suddenly. "John Dunn."

"Where does 'e live?" inquired the cook eagerly.

"Holebourne," said the old man—"a little place seven miles off the road."

"Are you sure it's the same," asked the cook in a trembling voice.

"Sartain," said the other firmly. "He come here first about six years ago, an' then he quarrelled with his landlord and went off to Holebourne."

The cook, with a flushed face, glanced along the quay to the schooner. Work was still proceeding amid a cloud of white dust, and so far his absence appeared to have passed unnoticed.

"If they want any dinner," he muttered, alluding to the powdered figures at work on the schooner, "they must get it for theirselves, that's all. Will you come and 'ave a drop, old man?"

The old man, nothing loath, assented, and having tasted of the cook's bounty, crawled beside him through the little town to put him on the road to Holebourne, and after seeing him safe, returned to his beloved post.

The cook went along whistling, thinking pleasantly of the discomfiture of the other members of the crew when they should discover his luck. For three miles he kept on sturdily, until a small signboard, projecting from between a couple of tall elms, attracted his attention to a little inn just off the road, at the porch of which a stout landlord sat on a wooden stool waiting for custom.

The cook hesitated a moment, and then marching slowly up, took a stool which stood opposite and ordered a pint.

The landlord rose and in a heavy, leisurely fashion, entered the house to execute the order, and returned carefully bearing a foaming mug.

"Take the top off," said the cook courteously.

The stout man, with a nod towards him, complied.

"'Ave a pint with me," said the cook, after a hasty glance into the interior, as the landlord handed him the mug. "You keep that one," he added.

The stout man drew another pint, and subsiding on to his stool with a little sigh, disposed himself for conversation.

"Taking a country walk?" he inquired.

The cook nodded. "Not all pleasure," he said importantly; "I'm on business."

"Ah, it's you fellows what make all the money," said the landlord. "I've only drawn these two pints this morning. Going far?"

"Holebourne," said the other.

"Know anybody there?" asked the landlord.

"Well, not exactly," said the cook; "I carn't say as I know 'im. I'm after a party o' the name o' Dunn."

"You won't get much out of him," said the landlady, who had just joined them. "He's a close un, he is."

The cook closed his eyes and smiled knowingly.

"There's a mystery about that man," said the landlady. "Nobody knows who he is or what he is, and he won't tell 'em. When a man's like that you generally know there's something wrong—leastways I do."

"Insulting, he is," said the landlord.

"Ah," said the cook, "'e won't insult me!"

"You know something about him?" said the landlady.

"A little," said the cook.

The landlord reached over to his wife, who bent her ear readily and dutifully towards him, and the cook distinctly caught the whispered word "'tec."

The landlady, after a curious glance at the cook, withdrew to serve a couple of wagoners who had drawn up at the door. Conversation became general, and it was evident that the wagoners shared the sentiments of the landlord and his wife with regard to Mr. Dunn. They regarded the cook with awe, and after proffering him a pint with respectful timidity, offered to give him a lift to Holebourne.

"I'd sooner go on my own," said the cook, with a glance at the wagons; "I want to get in the place quiet like and 'ave a look round before I do anythin'."

He sat there for some time resting, and evading as best he could the skilful questions of the landlady. The wagons moved off first, jolting and creaking their way to Holebourne, and the cook, after making a modest luncheon of bread and cheese and smoking a pipe, got on the road again.

"Look how he walks!" said the landlord, as the couple watched him up the road.

"Ah!" said his wife.

"Like a bloodhound," said the landlord impressively; "just watch him. I knew what he was directly I clapped eyes on him."

The cook continued his journey, unconscious of the admiration excited by his movements. He began to think that he had been a trifle foolish in talking so freely. Still, he had not said much, and if people liked to make mistakes, why, that was their business.

In this frame of mind he entered Holebourne, a small village consisting of a little street, an inn, and a church. At the end of the street, in front of a tidy little cottage with a well-kept front garden, a small knot of people were talking.

"Somethin' on," said the cook to himself as he returned with interest the stares of the villagers. "Which is Mr. Dunn's house, boy?"

"There it is, sir," said the boy, pointing to the house where the people were standing. "Are you the detective?"

"No," said the cook sharply.

He walked across to the house and opened the little garden gate, quite a little hum of excitement following him as he walked up to the door and knocked upon it with his knuckles.

"Come in," growled a deep voice.

The cook entered and carefully closed the door behind him. He found himself in a small sitting-room, the only occupant of which was an old man of forbidding aspect sitting in an easy chair with a newspaper open in his hand.

"What do you want?" he demanded, looking up.

"I want to see Mr. Dunn," said the cook nervously.

"I'm Mr. Dunn," said the other, waiting.

The cook's heart sank, for, with the exception of a beard, Mr. Dunn no more resembled the portrait than he did.

"I'm Mr. Dunn," repeated the old man, regarding him ferociously from beneath his shaggy eyebrows.

The cook smiled, but faintly. He tried to think, but the old man's gaze sent all the ideas out of his head.

"Oh, are you?" he said at length.

"I heard you were looking for me," said the old man, gradually raising his voice to a roar. "All the village knows it, I think, and now you've found me what the devil is it you want?"

"I—I think there's a mistake," stammered the cook.

"Oh," said the old man. "Ha! is there? Pretty detective you are. I'll bring an action against you. I'll have you imprisoned and dismissed the force."

"It's all a mistake," said the cook; "I'm not a detective."

"Come this way," said the old man, rising.

The cook followed him into a smaller room at the back.

"You're not a detective?" said the old man, as he motioned him to a seat. "I suppose you know that impersonating a detective is a serious offence? Just stay here while I fetch a policeman, will you?"

The cook said he wouldn't.

"Ah," said the old man with a savage grin, "I think you will." Then he went to the door and called loudly for "Roger."

Before the dazed cook of the Seamew could collect his scattered senses a pattering sounded on the stairs, and a bulldog came unobtrusively into the room. It was a perfectly bred animal, with at least a dozen points about it calling for notice and admiration, but all that the cook noticed was the excellent preservation of its teeth.

"Watch him, Roger," said the old man, taking a hat from a sideboard. "Don't let him move."

The animal growled intelligently, and sitting down a yard or two in front of the cook watched him with much interest.

"I'm sure I'm very sorry," muttered the cook. "Don't go away and leave me with this dog, sir."

"He won't touch you unless you move," said the old man.

The cook's head swam; he felt vaguely round for a subtle compliment. "I'd rather you stayed," he quavered, "I would indeed. I don't know any man I've took a greater fancy to at first sight."

"I don't want any of your confounded insolence," said the other sternly. "Watch him, Roger."

Roger growled with all the cheerfulness of a dog who had found a job which suited him, and his owner, after again warning the cook of what would happen if he moved out of the chair, left the room, shutting the door as he went. The cook heard the front door close behind him, and then all was silence, except for the strong breathing of Roger.

For some time the man and dog sat eyeing each other in silence, then the former, moistening his dry lips with his tongue, gave a conciliatory chirrup. Roger responded with a deep growl, and, rising to his feet, yawned expressively.

"Poor Roger!" said the cook in trembling accents, "poor old Rogy-wogy! Good old dog!"

The good old dog came a little nearer and closely inspected the cook's legs, which were knocking together with fright.

"Cats!" said the cook, pointing to the door as an idea occurred to him. "S-cat! Seize 'em, dog! seize 'em!"

"G-w-r-r," said Roger menacingly. The quivering limbs had a strange fascination for him, and coming closer he sniffed at them loudly.

In a perfect panic the cook, after glancing helplessly at the poker, put his hand gently behind him and drew his sheath-knife. Then, with a courage born of fear, he struck the dog suddenly in the body, and before it could recover from the suddenness of the attack, withdrew his knife and plunged it in again. The dog gave a choking growl and, game to the last, made a grab at the cook's leg, and missing it, rolled over on the floor, giving a faint kick or two as the breath left its body.

It had all happened so quickly that the cook, mechanically wiping his blade on the tablecloth, hardly realized the foulness of the crime of which he had been guilty, but felt inclined to congratulate himself upon his desperate bravery. Then as he realized that, in addition to the offence for which the choleric Mr. Dunn was even now seeking the aid of the law, there was a dead bulldog and a spoiled carpet to answer for, he resolved upon an immediate departure. He made his way to the back door, and sheathing his knife, crept stealthily down the garden, and clambered over the fence at the bottom. Then, with his back to the scene of the murder, he put up his hands and ran.

He crossed two fields and got on to a road, his breath coming painfully as he toiled along with an occasional glance behind him. It was uphill, but he kept on until he had gained the top, and then he threw himself down panting by the side of the road with his face turned in the direction of Holebourne. Five minutes later he started up again and resumed his flight, as several figures burst into the road from the village in hot pursuit.

For a little while he kept to the road, then, as the idea occurred to him that some of his pursuers might use a vehicle, he broke through the hedge and took to the fields. His legs gave way beneath him, and he stumbled rather than ran, but he kept on alternately walking and running until all signs of the pursuit had ceased.

CHAPTER IV

Safe for the time being, but with the memory of his offences pursuing him, the cook first washed his face and hands in a trough, and next removed the stains of the crime from his knife. He then pushed on again rapidly until he struck another road, and begging a lift from a passing wagon, lay full length on top of a load of straw and nervously scanned the landscape as they travelled. Half a dozen miles farther on the wagon halted before a comfortable farmhouse, and the cook, after bestowing on the carter two of the few coins left him, went his way, losing himself, with a view to baffling pursuit, among a maze of small lanes, turning right or left as the fancy took him, until nightfall found him tired and famished on the outskirts of a small village.

Conscious of the power of the telegraph, which he had no doubt was interesting itself in his behalf over the surrounding districts, he skulked behind a hedge until the lights went from the ground floor to the first floor of the cottages and then went out altogether. He then, with the utmost caution, looked round in search of shelter. He came at last to two cottages standing by themselves about half a mile beyond the village, one of which had a wooden shed in the garden which seemed to offer the very shelter he required. Satisfied that the inmates of the cottage were all abed he entered the garden, and, treading on tiptoe, walked towards the shed, fumbled at the hasp and opened the door. It was pitch dark within and silent, till something rustled uneasily. There was a note of alarm and indignation. The cook tripped on a stone, and only saved himself from falling by clutching at a perch which a dozen fowls instantly vacated with loud and frenzied appeals for assistance. Immediately the shed was full of flapping wings and agitated hens darting wildly between his legs as he made for the door again, only to run into the arms of a man who came from the cottage.

"I've got him, Poll!" shouted the latter, as he dealt the cook a blow with a stick. "I've got him!"

He fetched him another blow and was preparing, for a third, when the cook, maddened with the pain, struck at him wildly and sent him sprawling. He was up again in an instant and, aided by his wife, who had stopped to make a slight concession to appearances in the shape of a flannel petticoat, threw the cook down and knelt on him. A man came out from the adjoining cottage, and having, with great presence of mind, first found a vacant spot on the cook and knelt on it, asked what was the matter.

"After my hens," said the first man breathlessly. "I just heard 'em in time."

"I wasn't after your hens. I didn't know they was there!" gasped the cook.

"Lock him up!" said the second man warmly.

"I'm goin' to," said the other, "Keep still, you thief!"

"Get up!" said the cook faintly; "you're killin' me.

"Take him in the house and tie him up for the night, and we'll take him to Winton police station in the morning," said the neighbor. "He's a desperate character."

As they declined to trust the cook to walk, he was carried into the kitchen, where the woman, leaving him for a moment, struck a match and hastily lit a candle. She then opened a drawer and, to the cook's horror, began pulling out about twenty fathoms of clothes-line.

"The best way and the safest is to tie him in a chair," said the neighbor. "I remember my gran'-father used to tell a tale of how they served a highwayman that way once."

"That would be best, I think," said the woman pondering. "He'd be more comfortable in a chair, though I'm sure he don't deserve it."

They raised the exhausted cook, and placing him in a stout oak chair, lashed him to it until he could scarcely breathe.

"After my gran'father had tied the highwayman in the chair, he gave him a crack on the head with a stick," said the neighbor, regarding the cook thoughtfully.

"They was very brutal in those times," said the cook, before anybody else could speak.

"Just to keep him quiet like," said the neighbor, somewhat chilled by the silence of the other two.

"I think he'll do as he is," said the owner of the fowls, carefully feeling the prisoner's bonds. "If you'll come in in the morning, Pettit, we'll borrow a cart an' take him over to Winton. I expect there's a lot of things against him."

"I expect there is," said Pettit, as the cook shuddered. "Well, good-night."

He returned to his house, and the couple, after carefully inspecting the cook again, and warning him of the consequences if he moved, blew out the candle and returned to their interrupted slumbers.

For a long time the unfortunate cook sat in a state of dreary apathy, wondering vaguely at the ease with which he had passed from crime to crime, and trying to estimate how much he should get for each. A cricket sang from the hearthstone, and a mouse squeaked upon the floor. Worn out with fatigue and trouble, he at length fell asleep.

He awoke suddenly and tried to leap out of his bunk on to the floor and hop on one leg as a specific for the cramp. Then, as he realized his position, he strove madly to rise and straighten the afflicted limb. He was so far successful that he managed to stand, and in the fantastic appearance of a human snail, to shuffle slowly round the kitchen. At first he thought only of the cramp, but after that had yielded to treatment a wild idea of escape occurred to him. Still bowed with the chair, he made his way to the door, and, after two or three attempts, got the latch in his mouth and opened it. Within five minutes he had shuffled his way through the garden gate, which was fortunately open, and reached the road.

The exertion was so laborious that he sat down again upon his portable seat and reckoned up his chances. Fear lent him wings, though of a very elementary type, and as soon as he judged he was out of earshot he backed up against a tree and vigorously banged the chair against it.

He shed one cracked hind leg in this way, and the next time he sat down had to perform feats of balancing not unworthy of Blondin himself.

Until day broke did this persecuted man toil painfully along with the chair, and the sun rose and found him sitting carefully in the middle of the road, faintly anathematizing Captain Gething and everything connected with him. He was startled by the sound of footsteps rapidly approaching him, and, being unable to turn his head, he rose painfully to his feet and faced about bodily.

The new-comer stopped abruptly, and, gazing in astonishment at the extraordinary combination of man and chair before him, retired a few paces in disorder. At a little distance he had mistaken the cook for a lover of nature, communing with it at his ease; now he was undecided whether it was a monstrosity or an apparition.

"Mornin', mate," said the cook in a weary voice.

"Morning," said the man, backing still more.

"I 'spose," said the cook, trying to smile cheerfully, "you're surprised to see me like this?"

"I've never seen anything like it afore," said the man guardedly.

"I don't s'pose you 'ave," said the cook. "I'm the only man in England that can do it."

The man said he could quite believe it.

"I'm doin' it for a bet," said the cook.

"Oh-h," said the man, his countenance clearing, "a bet. I thought you were mad. How much is it?"

"Fifty pounds," said the cook. "I've come all the way from London like this."

"Well, I'm blest!" said the man. "What won't they think of next! Got much farther to go?"

"Oakville," said the cook, mentioning a place he had heard of in his wanderings. "At least I was, but I find it's too much for me. Would you mind doing me the favor of cutting this line?"

"No, no," said the other reproachfully, "don't give up now. Why, it's only another seventeen miles."

"I must give it up," said the cook, with a sad smile.

"Don't be beat," said the man warmly. "Keep your 'art up, and you'll be as pleased as Punch presently to think how near you was losing."

"Cut it off," said the cook, trembling with impatience; "I've earned forty pounds of it by coming so far. If you cut it off I'll send you ten of it."

The man hesitated while an inborn love of sport struggled with his greed.

"I've got a wife and family," he said at last in extenuation, and taking out a clasp-knife, steadied the cook with one hand while he severed his bonds with the other.

"God bless you, mate!" said the cook, trying to straighten his bowed back as the chair fell to the ground.

"My name's Jack Thompson," said his benefactor. "Jack Thompson, Winchgate 'll find me."

"I'll make it twelve pounds," said the grateful cook, "and you can have the chair."

He shook him by the hand, and, freed from his burden, stepped out on his return journey, while his innocent accomplice, shouldering the chair, went back to learn from the rightful owner a few hard truths about his mental capacity.

Not knowing how much start he would have, the cook, despite his hunger and fatigue, pushed on with all the speed of which he was capable. After an hour's journey he ventured to ask the direction of an embryo ploughman, and wheedled out of him a small, a very small, portion of his breakfast. From the top of the next hill he caught a glimpse of the sea, and taking care to keep this friend of his youth in sight, felt his way along by it to Brittlesea. At midday he begged some broken victuals from a gamekeeper's cottage, and with renewed vigor resumed his journey, and at ten o'clock that night staggered on to Brittlesea quay and made his way cautiously to the ship. There was nobody on deck, but a light burned in the foc'sle, and after a careful peep below he descended. Henry, who was playing, a losing game of draughts with Sam, looked up with a start, and overturned the board.

"Lord love us, cookie!" said Sam, "where 'ave you been?"

The cook straightened up, smiling faintly, and gave a wave of his hand which took in all the points of the compass. "Everywhere," he said wearily.

"You've been on the spree," said Sam, regarding him severely.

"Spree!" said the cook with expression. "Spree!"

His feelings choked him, and after a feeble attempt to translate them into words, he abandoned the attempt, and turning a deaf ear to Sam's appeal for information, rolled into his bunk and fell fast asleep.

CHAPTER V

They got under way at four o'clock next morn-ing, and woke the cook up to assist at 3.30. At 3.45 they woke him again, and at 3.50 dragged him from his bunk and tried to arouse him to a sense of his duties. The cook, with his eyes still closed, crawled back again the moment they left him, and though they had him out twice after that, he went back in the same somnambulistic state and resumed his slumbers.

Brittlesea was thirty miles astern when he at length awoke and went on deck, and the schooner was scudding along under a stiff breeze. It was a breeze such as the mate loved, and his face was serene and peaceful until his gaze fell upon the shrinking figure of the cook as it glided softly into the galley.

"Cook," he roared, "come here, you skulking rascal! Where've you been all this time?"

"I've been in trouble, sir," said the cook humbly; "you'll 'ardly believe the trouble I've been in through trying to do the skipper a kindness."

"Don't you come none of that with me," roared the mate warningly. "Where've you been? Come, out with it!"

The cook, still somewhat weak from his adventures, leaned against the companion, and with much dramatic gesture began his story. As it proceeded the mate's breath came thick and fast, his color rose, and he became erratic in his steering. Flattered by these symptoms of concern, the cook continued.

"That'll do," said the mate at last.

"I ain't got to the worst of it yet, sir," said the cook.

"If you stand there lying to me for another moment I'll break your neck," said the mate violently. "You've had two days on the drink, that's what you've had."

"It's gawspel truth, sir," said the cook solemnly.

"You wait till the skipper turns out," said the other, shaking his fist at him. "If it wasn't for leaving the wheel I'd set about you myself, my lad."

To the cook's indignation the skipper shared the opinions of the mate concerning his story, and in a most abrupt and unfeeling fashion stopped two days' pay. Down in the foc'sle he fared no better, the crew's honest tribute of amazement to his powers of untruthful narrative passing all bounds of decorum.

Their incredulity was a source of great grief to him. He had pictured himself posing as a daredevil, and he went about his duties with a chastened mien, mistaken by the men, experts in such matters, for the reaction after a drinking bout.

They passed Northfleet on their way up to Rotherhithe, where they went to discharge a small general cargo, the cook's behavior every time a police-boat passed them coming in for much scornful censure. It was some hours before he would go ashore, and when at last he did venture, it was with the reckless air of a Robert Macaire and a Dick Turpin rolled into one.

It was a damp, cheerless morning when they got to Northfleet again. It had been raining heavily in the night, and black clouds still hung low over the river. They were not to load until the next day, and after dinner Henry and the mate exchanged a sympathetic smile as the skipper took up his cap and went ashore.

He walked into Gravesend, and taking no notice of the rain, which was falling steadily, strolled idly about looking into the shop windows. He had a romantic idea that he might meet Annis Gething there. It was half-holiday at the school, and it was the most natural thing in the world that she should be sauntering about Gravesend in the pouring rain. At about four o'clock, being fairly wet through, he saw the fallacy of the idea strongly, and in a disconsolate fashion, after one glass at a convenient tavern, turned to go back to the ship. A little way along the road he stepped aside to allow a girl to pass, glancing—by mere force of habit—beneath her umbrella as he did so. Then he started back guiltily as his eyes met those of Miss Gething. She half stopped.

"Good-afternoon," said the skipper awkwardly.

"Good-afternoon," said she.

"Nasty weather," said the skipper, standing respectfully three yards off.

"Wretched," said Miss Gething. "Ugh!"

"I don't mind it much myself," said the skipper.

"You must be very wet," said Miss Gething. "You are going to see mother, I suppose?"

"I did think of doing so," said the skipper with joyous untruthfulness.

"I'm going to do a little shopping," said she. "Good-bye."

She nodded brightly, and the skipper, raising his cap, turned on his heel and set off to pay the call. He turned his head several times as he went, but Miss Gething, who knew more of men than the skipper knew of women, did not turn hers.

A quarter of an hour's brisk walk brought him to the house, and he shook the rain from his cap as he knocked gently at the door. It was opened by a man, who, standing with his hand on the lock regarded him inquiringly.

"Mrs. Gething in?" asked the skipper.

"No, she's not just at present," said the other.

"I'll come in and wait for her if you don't mind," said the skipper, speaking on the spur of the moment.

The other hesitated, and then standing aside to allow him to pass, closed the door, and they entered the small parlor together. The skipper, with a courage which surprised himself, took a chair uninvited and began to wipe his trousers with his handkerchief.

"I'm afraid Mrs. Gething will be a long time," said the other man at last.

"I'll give her a few minutes," said the skipper, who would have sat there a week with pleasure.

He rubbed his moustache and beard with his handkerchief and put them into shape with his fingers. The other man regarded these operations with an unfavorable eye, and watched him uneasily.

"No message you could leave for Mrs. Gething," he suggested, after a quarter of an hour.

The skipper shook his head, and in his turn took stock of the other man—a good-looking fellow with a waxed black moustache, a light silk tie and a massive scarf-pin. A frock-coat hung about his knees, and shoes of the lightest brown called attention to his small feet.

Another quarter of an hour passed. "Wet day," said the skipper, by way of starting the conversation again.

The other assented, and remarked that he thought it very probable that the wet would prevent Mrs. Gething from returning, whereupon conversation languished until the sound of hurried footsteps outside, and the turning of a key in the latch, made them both look up.

"Here she is," said the skipper softly.

The other man said nothing, feeling possibly that the entrance of Miss Gething was sufficient refutation of the statement. He was also in anything but a talkative mood.

"Mother not in?" said Miss Gething in surprise as she entered the room. "How good of you to wait, captain."

"Oh, it's no trouble," said the skipper, who really thought that there was no credit due to him for his action.

She shook hands with the other man and smiled at the skipper. "I've seen you before," she said, "and it is good of you to wait. I'm sure you're very wet. This is Mr. Glover, Captain Wilson."

The two gentlemen glared their acknowledgments, and the skipper, with a sinking at his heart, began to feel in the way. Miss Gething, after going outside to remove her hat and jacket, came in smiling pleasantly, and conversation became general, the two men using her as a sort of human telephone through which to transmit scanty ideas.

"Half-past five," said Miss Gething suddenly. "Have you got to catch the 6.30 train, Mr. Glover?"

"Must," said Mr. Glover dismally. "Business, you know," he added resignedly.

"You'll take a cup of tea before you go?" said Annis.

She was standing before Mr. Glover as she spoke, and the skipper, who had been feeling more and more in the way, rose and murmured that he must go. His amazement when Miss Gething twisted her pretty face into a warning scowl and shook her head at him, was so great that Mr. Glover turned suddenly to see the cause of it.

"You'll take a cup, too, captain?" said Miss Gething with a polite smile.

"Thank you," said the skipper, resuming his seat. His ideas were in a whirl, and he sat silent as the girl deftly set the tea-table and took her seat before the tray.

"Quite a tea-party," she said brightly. "One piece of sugar, Mr. Glover?"

"Two," said the gentleman in an injured voice.

She looked inquiringly at the skipper with the sugar-tongs poised.

"I'll leave it to you," said he confusedly. Mr. Glover smiled contemptuously, and raised his eye-brows a little. Miss Gething dropped in one piece and handed him the cup.

"Sometimes I take one piece, sometimes two or three," said the skipper, trying to explain away his foolishness. "I'm not particular."

"You must be of an easy-going nature," said Miss Gething indulgently.

"Don't know his own mind, I should think," said Mr. Glover rudely.

"I know it about other things," said the skipper.

The tone in which this remark was made set Mr. Glover wondering darkly what the other things were. Neither man was disposed to be talkative, and tea would have proceeded in sombre silence but for the hostess. At ten minutes past six Mr. Glover rose and with great unwillingness said he must go.

"It isn't raining much now," said Miss Gething encouragingly. Mr. Glover went to the hall, and taking his hat and umbrella, shook hands with her. Then he came to the door again, and looked at the skipper. "Going my way?" he inquired with great affability, considering.

"Er—no," said the other.

Mr. Glover put on his hat with a bang, and with a curt nod followed Miss Gething to the door and departed.

"I think he'll catch the train all right," said the skipper, as Miss Gething watched his feverish haste from the window.

"I hope so," said she.

"I'm sorry your mother wasn't in," said the skipper, breaking a long pause.

"Yes, it has been dull for you, I'm afraid," said the girl.

The skipper sighed wearily and wondered whether Mr. Glover was such an adept at silly remarks as he appeared to be.

"Has he got far to go?" he inquired, referring to Mr. Glover.

"London," said Annis briefly.

She stood at the window for some time, gazing up the road with what appeared to be an expression of anxious solicitude.

"Well, I suppose I must be going," said the skipper, who thought he ought not to stay any longer.

Annis stood aside as he rose, and followed him slowly to the hall.

"I wish we had an umbrella to lend you," she said, looking round.

"Oh, that'll be all right," said the skipper. "I'm nearly dry now."

"Dry?" said Annis. She put her little hand on his coat-sleeve.

"Oh, you're soaking," she said in dismay. "The idea of me letting you sit about in that state!"

"That sleeve is the worst," said the skipper, whom circumstances had made artful. "It's all right here."

He brushed his hand down his coat.

"That's a good thing," said Annis politely.

"Um, but not here," said the skipper, squeezing the lapel of his coat.

Annis touched his coat lightly.

"You're very wet," she said severely; "you ought not to sit about in such things. Wait a moment. I'll get you a great-coat of my father's."

She sped lightly up the stairs, and returning with a long, heavy coat, held it out to him.

"That'll keep you dry," she remarked as the skipper, after a few slight remonstrances, began to put it on. She held the other sleeve up for him and watched, with the satisfaction of a philanthropist, as he buttoned it up. Then she opened the door.

"You'll give my respects to Mrs. Gething?" said the skipper.

"Certainly. She'll be sorry she wasn't in. Are you staying here long?"

"About three days."

Annis pondered.

"She's going out to-morrow," she said tentatively.

"I shall be in the town the day after on business," said the skipper. "If it wouldn't be troubling you I might look in. Good-bye."

He shook hands confusedly, wondering whether he had gone too far; and, as the door closed behind him, put his hands in Captain Gething's pockets and went off in a brown study. Slowly and distinctly as he went along the various things grouped themselves together in his mind, and he began to think aloud.

"She knew her mother was out when she met me," he said slowly. "She knew that other fellow was here; but one would have thought—Lovers' tiff," he said suddenly and bitterly; "and doing the pleasant to me to make him smart a bit. He'll be round to-morrow when the mother's out."

He went back dejectedly to his ship, and countermanding the tea with which the zealous Henry was about to indulge him, changed his clothes and sat down to smoke.

"You've got a bit wet," said the mate. "Where'd you get the coat?"

"Friend," said the other. "Had it lent to me. You know that Captain Gething I told you to look out for?"

"I do," said the other eagerly.

"Let the crew know that the reward is raised to five pounds," said the skipper, drawing strongly at his pipe.

"If the reward is riz to five pounds the cook'll be 'ung for murder or som'think," said Henry. "It's no use lookin' to the crew for 'elp, sir—not a bit."

The skipper deigned no reply, and his message having been conveyed to the foc'sle, a scene of intense animation prevailed there.

"I'm goin' to have a go now," said Dick emphatically. "Five pounds is worth picking up."

"I only 'ope as you won't 'ave the treat I 'ad," said the cook feelingly.

"Wot we want," said fat Sam, "is one o' them things people 'ave in the City—one o' the 'er what d'yer call 'ems."

"'Ansom keb?" suggested the cook.

"'Ansom keb be damned!" said Sam scornfully.

"One of them things wot 'as a lot o' people in, I mean."

"Tramcars," said the cook, who was all at sea. "But you couldn't take a tramcar all over the country, Sam."

"If anybody was to ask me, I should say you was a silly fool," said Sam impatiently. "I mean one o' them things people puts their money in."

The wondering cook had got as far as "automatic mach—" when Henry jostled him into silence.

"Wot are you gettin' at?" said Dick. "Why don't you talk plain?"

"'Cos I can't remember the word," said Sam angrily; "but a lot o' people gets together and goes shares."

"You mean a syndikit," said Dick.

"That's the word," said Sam, with relief.

"Well, wot's the good of it?" said Dick.

"This way," said Sam; "we make up a syndikit and divide the money when 'e's found. It 'ud be a cruel thing, Dick, if, just as you'd spotted your man, I wos to come along and snap 'im up under your werry nose, for instance—"

"You'd better try it," said Dick grimly.

"It's a very good idea o' yours, Sam," said the cook. "I'll join it."

"You'd better come in, Dick," said Sam.

"Not me," said Dick; "it's five pounds I'm after."

"We shall beworkin' agin you, you know, me an' the cook an' the boy," said Sam anxiously.

"Ho!" said Henry, "don't think I'm takin' a 'and, cos I'm not."

"Werry good, then," said Sam, "the—the—what d'ye call it, Dick?"

"Syndikit," said Dick.

"The syndikit is me and the cook, then," said Sam. "Give us your 'and, cook."

In this informal way the "Captain Gething Search Company" was founded, and the syndicate, thinking that they had a good thing, began to hold aloof from their fellows, and to confer darkly in remote corners. They expended a shilling on a popular detective story entitled, "On the Trail," and an element of adventure was imported into their lives which brightened them considerably.

The following day the skipper spent hard at work with the cargo, bustling about with feverish energy as the afternoon wore on and left him to imagine his rival tête-à-tête with Annis. After tea a reaction set in, and, bit by bit the mate, by means of timely sympathy, learnt all that there was to know. Henry, without a display of anything, except, perhaps, silence, learnt it too.

"It's in your favor that it's your own craft," said the mate; "you can go where you like. If you find the father, she might chuck the other feller."

"That isn't my object in finding him," said the skipper. "I just want to find him to oblige her."

He set off the following afternoon followed by the stealthy glances of the crew, who had heard something from Henry, and, first getting his beard trimmed at a barber's, walked along to call on Mrs. Gething. She was in, and pleased to see him, and hearing that his crew were also searching, supplied him with another photograph of the missing captain.

"Miss Gething well?" inquired the skipper as, after accepting an invitation to a cup of tea, he noticed that she only laid for two.

"Oh, yes; she's gone to London," said Mrs. Gething. "She's got friends there, you know."

"Mr. Glover," said the skipper to himself with dismal intuition. "I met a friend here the day before yesterday," he said aloud.

"Oh, yes—Mr. Glover," said the old lady; "a man in a very good position. He's very nice, isn't he?"

"Splendid," murmured the skipper vaguely.

"He would do anything for her," said the fond mother. "I'm sure it's quite touching the way he looks after her."

"Going to be married soon?" queried the skipper.

He knew it was a rude question for a comparative stranger to ask, but he couldn't help it.

"When my husband is found," said the old lady, shaking her head sadly. "She won't marry till then."

The skipper sat back in his chair, and pushing his plate from him, pondered over this latest piece of information. It seemed at first an excellent reason for not finding Captain Gething, but the idea had hardly occurred to him before he dismissed it as unworthy, and manfully resolved to do his best. For an hour he sat listening to the somewhat prosy talk of the old lady, and then—there being no sign of Annis's return—he silently departed and made his way back to the Seamew.

CHAPTER VI

To the cook's relief he found that the Seamew's next voyage was to a little port on the West Coast named Cocklemouth, calling at the garrison town of Bymouth on the way. He told Sam that it was a load off his mind, and showed clearly by his manner that he expected the syndicate at least to accept his story. They spent most of their time in the galley, where, secure from money-grubbing eavesdroppers, they matured their plans over the washing of potatoes and the scouring of saucepans. "On the Trail" was remarkably clever, and they obtained many helpful suggestions from it, though the discovery that Henry had got hold of it, and had marked all the most valuable passages in lead pencil, caused them much anxiety.

The syndicate were the first to get ashore the evening they arrived at Bymouth. They had come to the conclusion in their deliberations that the only possible place in which a retired mariner would spend his evenings was a public-house, and they resolved to do them thoroughly.

"The worst of it," said Sam, as they walked slowly together to the town, "is the drinkin'. Arter I've 'ad five or six pints, everybody looks to me like Cap'n Gething."

"We won't 'ave no drinkin'," said the cook. "We'll do wot the feller did in that story. 'Ave you got sixpence about you?"

"Wot for?" inquired Sam carefully.

"Workin' expenses," replied the cook, dwelling fondly on the phrase.

"That'll be thruppence each, then," said Sam, eyeing him suspiciously.

"Sixpence each," said the cook. "Now do you know what we're goin' to do?"

"Chuck money away," hazarded Sam as he reluctantly drew a sixpence from his pocket and handed it to the cook. "Where's your sixpence?"

The cook showed it to him, and Sam, whose faith in human nature had been largely shaken by a perusal of the detective story referred to, bit it critically.

"We can't go into pubs without drinkin' in the ordinary way," said the cook, "so we're goin' in to sell bootlaces, like the chap in the book did. Now do you see?"

"Why not try something cheaper first?" growled Sam—"measurin' footmarks, or over-'earing fellers talking? It's just like you, cookie, doin' expensive things."

Under the cook's glance of silent scorn he became first restive and then abusive, winding up finally by demanding his money back.

"Don't you be a fool!" said the cook coarsely. "You leave it to me."

"And get tied up in a chair with my own bootlaces p'raps," said the irritated seaman.

The cook, affecting not to hear him, looked out for a boot-shop, and having found one, walked in, followed by the discontented Sam, and purchased a shilling's-worth of laces.

"Wot am I to say?" demanded Sam surlily, as they stood outside, and the cook hung half a dozen laces over his arm.

"You needn't say anything," replied the cook. "Just walk in an' 'old 'em up in the people's faces, an' if anybody offers you a drink you may 'ave it."

"Thank you for nothin'," said Sam, with prophetic insight.

"You take all the pubs this side of the 'igh Street an' I'll take the other," said the cook. "And if you look as cheerful as you look now you ought to take a lot o' money."

He turned away, and with a farewell caution against drinking, set off. The stout seaman, with a strong distaste for his job, took the laces in his hand and bent his steps in the direction of a small but noisy tavern in the next street. The public bar was full, and Sam's heart failed him as he entered it, and, bearing the cook's instructions in mind, held up his wares to the customers. Most of them took no notice, and the only man who said anything to him was a red-nosed sergeant of marines, who, setting his glass with great deliberation on the counter, gazed fixedly at a dozen laces crawling over his red sleeve. His remarks, when he discovered their connection with Sam, were of a severe and sweeping character, and contained not the slightest reference to a drink.

In the next bar he met a philanthropist who bought up his whole stock-in-trade. The stout seaman was utterly unprepared for such kindness, and stood looking at him dumbly, his lips all a-tremble with naughty words.

"There, there," said his benefactor kindly. "Never mind about thanking me."

Sam obeyed him easily, and departing in silence, went off raving to the nearest boot-shop to buy more laces. Taught by experience, he put some of his new stock in his pocket, and with a couple of pairs in his hand, entered the next tavern on his beat.

The bar was pretty full, but he pushed his way in, and offering his wares in a perfunctory fashion, looked round carefully for any signs of Captain Gething.

"Outside!" said a smart barmaid with a toss of her head as she caught sight of him.

"I'm goin', miss," said Sam, blushing with shame. Hitherto most barmaids had treated him with kindness, and in taverns where his powers were known, usually addressed him as "sir."

"Down on your luck, mate?" said a voice as he turned to go.

"Starvin', sir," said Sam, who was never one to trouble about appearances.

"Sit down," said his new friend, with a nod at the barmaid, who was still regarding the seaman in a hostile fashion.

Sam sat down and mentally blessed the reservation regarding free drinks as his benefactor turned to the bar and gave his order. His eyes beamed softly with a mixture of gratitude and amusement as his new friend came back with a pint of ale and half a loaf of bread.

"Get through that, old chap," said the man as he handed him the bread; "and there's some more where that came from."

He sat down opposite, and taking a long pull at the pewter, watched with a kind smile to see the famished seaman eat. He noted as a strange fact that starving men nibble gently at the outside crust first, and then start on small, very small, mouthfuls of crumb, instinct rather than reason probably warning them of the dangers of a surfeit.

For a few minutes Sam, with one eye on the pewter and the other on the door, struggled to perform his part. Then he rose, and murmuring broken thanks, said he would take some home to his wife and children.

"Never mind your wife and children," said his benefactor, putting down the empty pewter. "You eat that up and I'll give you a couple of loaves to take home to them."

"My 'art's too full to eat," said Sam, getting a little nearer the door.

"He means his stomach," said a stern but youthful voice which the unhappy seaman knew only too well. He turned smartly and saw the face of Henry peering over the partition, and beside it the grinning countenance of Dick.

"He was on our ship this afternoon," continued his youthful tormentor as he scrambled still higher up the partition, and getting one arm over, pointed an accusing finger at Sam, who had been pushed back into his seat. "We gave him a lovely dinner, an' arter he'd eat it he went off on the quiet in one of our chaps' clothes."

"That's right, mates," said the delighted Dick, nodding at the audience.

"One of our chaps named Sam," went on Henry—"one of the best an' kindest 'earted chaps that ever breathed."

"Regular brick he is," assented Dick.

"Fine, big 'ansome man, he is," said Henry, "and this chap's got his clothes on."

The customers gazed sternly at Sam as he sat open-mouthed listening to these fulsome but untimely praises. In every gathering there is sure to be one or two whose self-imposed mission it is to right wrongs, and one of this type present at once suggested returning the clothes to the rightful owner. His suggestion was adopted with enthusiasm, and a dozen men closed round the hapless Sam.

"Outside, gentlemen, please," said the barmaid hastily.

They went out in a cluster, the stout seaman in the centre fighting like a madman, and nearly overturning three soldiers who were passing. Two of them were named Murphy and one O'Sullivan, and the riot that ensued took three policemen and a picket to subdue. Sam, glad of a chance to get away, only saw the beginning of it, and consumed by violent indignation, did not pause until he had placed half a dozen streets between himself and the scene of his discomfiture.

He had no intention of breaking faith with the cook, but he had a pint and thought that circumstances justified it. Then he walked slowly up and down the street a little while, debating whether he should continue the search or return to the schooner. For a time he strolled on aimlessly, and then, resolving not to be defeated by the impertinences of Dick and the boy, paused before a high-class tavern and went in. Two or three well-dressed men, whose behavior contrasted favorably with that of the vulgar crew he had just left, shook their heads, but not unkindly, and he was about to leave when a big, black-bearded man entered.

"That's a poor game," said the big man, glancing at the laces.

"Yes, sir," said Sam humbly.

"You look as if you thrive on it," said the man, somewhat sternly.

"It's only looks, sir," said Sam, shaking his head as he walked to the door.

"Drink, I s'pose," said the other.

"No, sir," said Sam.

"When did you taste food last?" continued the other.

"Yesterday morning," said Sam, clearing a soft piece of bread from his teeth with his tongue.

"Could you take something?" inquired the other.

Sam smiled expectantly and took a seat. He heard his new friend order a pot, and wiping his mouth on the back of his hand, tried to think of something nice to say as he drank it. Then his blood froze in his veins, and his jaw dropped as the other came from the counter and held out half a loaf.

"There, my man," he said kindly, "put that inside you."

Sam took it and tried to put it into his pocket, and repeating his old tale about taking it home to the children, rose to depart.

"You eat that, and I'll give you a couple of loaves to take home to them," said the other.

The bread fell from Sam's nerveless fingers and rolled on to the floor. A bystander picked it up, and wiping it on his coat, returned it to him.

"Go on," said the big man, taking a deep draught of his beer—"eat away."

"I must see my children eat first," said Sam in a broken voice.

"You eat that bread or I'll call a policeman and give you in charge," said the other, raising his voice. "I believe you're an impostor. Where's your hawker's license?"

In a state bordering upon frenzy Sam bit off a piece of the bread and tried to swallow it. He took up a water-bottle and drank some of the contents, and within five minutes had swallowed as many mouthfuls.

"Go on," said the donor sternly.

"I won't," said Sam fiercely; "damned if I will!"

The other rose and went to the door. "Just step this way a minute, constable," he said quietly.

He stood aside, and, as Sam paused with the bread in his hand, the door opened and Dick and Henry entered, and shaking their heads, gazed sorrowfully upon him. The big man sat down and laughed until he cried as Sam, realizing the plot of which he had been the victim, flung the bread at Henry and made for the door. He went down the road mad with indignation, and with a firm resolve to have no more to do with bootlaces, pitched them away.

"Hallo, Sam!" cried a figure from the other side of the road. "Any luck?"

Sam shook his head speechlessly.

"You've been drinkin," said the cook as he came over.

"I ain't," said Sam. Then a base idea occurred to him, and he took the other by the arm.

"There's a pub down here, cook," he said in a trembling voice, "an' there's an old chap there I can't be certain of. S'pose you go an' have a look at 'im."

"Which one?" inquired his innocent friend.

Full of a great joy, Sam led him to the place of his mortification, and waiting until he was fairly in, stood listening behind the door.

"Why don't they speak up?" he said crossly, as a low, indistinct murmuring reached him. He strained his ears intently, but could not catch anything, and losing all patience, was just about to push the door open and peep in when he heard a roar of laughter. Peal upon peal sounded until the bar shook with it, and an expression of peace and rest came over his face as he pictured the scene inside.

"Don't," said the cook's voice feebly.

There was another roar of laughter, to which Sam grinned a silent accompaniment.

"You'll kill me," said the cook again, in a choking voice.

"No worse for you than for me, my lad," said Sam, with great content.

There was another roar in which Sam, to his amazement, fancied that the cook joined. He was still listening in a state of maddening perplexity when he heard the cook's voice again.

"Poor old Sam!" it said distinctly. "Poor old Sam! I'd 'ave given anythin' to 'ave seen him."

The listener stiffened up suddenly and, holding his breath, went off on tiptoe down the street, the sounds of the foolish mirth in the bar ringing in his ears as he went. His brain was in a whirl, but two definite objects shaped themselves in his mind as he walked fiercely on—to smash first the syndicate, and then the cook. With these ideas firmly fixed he went aboard again, and going into the lonely foc'sle, climbed into his bunk and forgot his sorrows in sleep—in a sleep so sound that the others, upon their return an hour later, failed to wake him, until Henry, as a last expedient, threw a slice of bread at him. After which everybody had to keep awake all night to mount guard over their lives.

CHAPTER VII

The search at Bymouth obtained no further assistance from Sam. For the remainder of their stay there he hardly moved from the ship, preferring to smoke his pipe in peace on board to meeting certain jocular spirits ashore who wanted to buy bootlaces. Conversation with Dick and the boy he declined altogether, and it was not until they had reached Cocklemouth that he deigned to accept a pipe of tobacco from the cook's box.

Cocklemouth is a small lone place on the Welsh coast. When a large ship gets into the tiny harbor the inhabitants come down to see it, and the skippers of small craft pop up from their cabins and yell out to know where it's coming to. Even when they see it bound and guided by many hawsers they are not satisfied, but dangling fenders in an obtrusive fashion over the sides of their ships, prepare for the worst.

"We won't find 'im 'ere, cookie," said Sam, as the syndicate sat on deck on the evening of their arrival gazing contemplatively at the few scattered lights which appeared as twilight deepened into night. "Lonesome little place."

"I ain't got much 'ope of finding 'im anywhere," assented the cook.

"If it wasn't for fear of Dick finding 'im," said Sam viciously, "or the boy, I'd just give it up, cookie."

"If anybody finds 'im it'll be the skipper hisself," said the cook, lowering his voice as the person alluded to passed them on his way ashore. "He goes to the police station with the portrait and arsts them there. What chance 'ave we got after that?"

The seaman shook his head, and after sitting for some time in silence, went ashore with the cook and drank himself into a state of hopeless pessimism. In this condition he forgave everybody, and feeling very low, made his will by the simple process of giving his knife to Dick and two and sevenpence to Henry. The trouble he had in revoking it next morning furnished a striking illustration of the depths to which poor humanity can descend.

It was bright and fine next day, and after breakfast his spirits rose. The persistent tinkle of a cracked bell from a small brick church in the town, and the appearance of two girls walking along the quay with hymn-books, followed by two young men without, reminded him that it was Sunday.

The skipper, who was endeavoring to form new habits, obeyed the summons of the bell. The mate took a healthful walk of three miles, while the crew sat about the deck watching the cook's preparations for dinner, and occasionally lending him some slight assistance. It was not until the meal was despatched that they arrayed themselves in their Sunday clothes and went ashore.

Dick went first, having thoughtfully provided himself with the photograph which had been lent for the use of all of them. He walked at first into the town, but the bare shuttered shops and deserted streets worked upon his feelings, and with his hands in his pockets, he walked back in the direction of the harbor. Here he got into conversation with an elderly man of sedate aspect, and after a little general talk, beginning with the weather and ending with tobacco, he produced the photograph and broached the subject of Captain Gething.

"Well, I've seen a man very much like it," said his new friend after a prolonged study.

"Where?" asked Dick eagerly.

"I won't say it's the same man," said the other slowly, as he handed the portrait back, "but if it ain't him it's his brother."

"Where?" repeated Dick impatiently.

"Well, I don't know that I ought to interfere," said the man; "it ain't my business."

"If a bob would—" began Dick.

"It would," said the man, smiling as he pocketed it. "He lives at Piggott's Bay," he said impressively.

"And where might that be?" inquired the seaman.

The man turned and pointed across a piece of untidy waste ground to a coastguard's path which wound its way along the top of the cliffs.

"Follow that path as straight as you can go," said he.

"How far?" said Dick.

"Well, some people make a long journey of it, and some a short one," said the other oracularly. "Shall we say six miles?"

Dick said he would sooner say three.

"An easy six, then," said the man smiling indulgently. "Well, good-day to you."

"Good-day, mate," said Dick, and plunging into the débris before him, started on his walk.

It was unfortunate for him in the sequel that Sam and the cook, who had started out for a quiet stroll, without any intention of looking for Captain Gething, or any nonsense of that kind, had witnessed the interview from a distance. By dint of hurrying they overtook the elderly man of sedate aspect, and by dint of cross-questioning, elicited the cause of Dick's sudden departure.

"Which way is it?" inquired Sam.

"You follow him," said the man, indicating the figure in front as it slowly ascended the cliff, "and you'll be there as soon as he will."

The comfortable stroll was abandoned, and the couple, keeping at a respectful distance, followed their unconscious comrade. The day was hot, and the path, which sometimes ran along the top of the cliff and sometimes along the side of it, had apparently escaped the attention of the local County Council. No other person was in sight, and the only things that moved were a few sheep nibbling the short grass, which scampered off at their approach, and a gull or two poised overhead.

"We want to get there afore 'e does," said Sam, treading gingerly along a difficult piece of path.

"He'd see us if we ran along the beach," said the cook.

"We can't run on shingle," said Sam; "and it don't seem much good just gettin' there to see 'im find the cap'n, does it?"

"We must wait for an hoppertunity," said the cook.

Sam grunted.

"An' when it comes, seize it at once," continued the cook, who disapproved of the grunt.

They kept on for some time steadily, though Sam complained bitterly about the heat as he mopped his streaming brow.

"He's going down on to the beach," said the cook suddenly. "Make a spurt for it, Sam, and we'll pass him."

The stout seaman responded to the best of his ability, and arriving at the place where Dick had disappeared, flung himself down on the grass and lay there panting. He was startled by a cry of surprise from the cook.

"Come on, Sam," he said eagerly; "he's going in for a swim."

His friend moved to the edge of the cliff and looked over. A little heap of clothing lay just below him, and Dick was striding over the sands to the sea.

"Come on," repeated the cook impatiently; "we've got the start."

"I should laugh if somebody was to steal his clothes," said Sam vindictively as he gazed at the garments.

"Be all right for us if they did," said the cook; "we'd have plenty o' time to look around this 'ere Piggott's Bay then." He glanced at Sam as he spoke, and read his horrible purpose in his eyes. "No, no!" he said hastily.

"Not steal 'em, cookie," said Sam seductively, "only bury 'em under the shingle. I'll toss you who does it."

For sixty seconds the cook struggled gamely with the tempter.

"It's just a bit of a joke, cook," said Sam jovially. "Dick 'ud be the first to laugh at it hisself if it was somebody else's clothes." He spun a penny in the air, and covering it deftly, held it out to the cook.

"Heads!" said the latter softly.

"Tails!" said Sam cheerfully; "hurry up, cook."

The cook descended without a word, and hastily interring the clothes, not without an uneasy glance seaward, scrambled up the cliff again and rejoined his exultant accomplice. They set off in silence, keeping at some distance from the edge of the cliff.

"Business is business," said the cook after a time, "and he wouldn't join the syndikit."

"He was greedy, and wanted it all," said Sam with severity.

"P'raps it'll be a lesson to 'im," said the cook unctuously. "I took the bearings of the place in case 'e don't find 'em. Some people wouldn't ha' done that."

They kept on steadily for another hour, until at last they came quite suddenly upon a little fishing village situated on a tiny bay. Two or three small craft were anchored inside the stone pier, along which two or three small children, in all the restriction of Sunday clothes, were soberly pacing up and down.

"This must be it," said Sam. "Keep your eyes open, cook."

"What's the name o' this place, mate?" said Sam expectantly to an old salt who was passing.

"Stone-pen Quay," said the old man.

Sam's face fell. "How far is it to Piggott's Bay, then?" he inquired.

"To where?" said the old man, taking his pipe out of his mouth and staring hard.

"Piggott's Bay," said Sam.

"You don't tell me you're looking for Piggott's Bay," said the old man.

"Why not?" said Sam shortly.

Instead of replying the old man slapped his leg, and with his pipe cocked at one side of his mouth, laughed a thin senile laugh with the other.

"When you've done laughin'," said the cook with dignity.

"But I ain't," said the old man, removing his pipe and laughing with greater freedom. "They're looking for Piggott's Bay, Joe," he said, turning to a couple of fishermen who had just come up.

"What a lark!" said Joe, beaming with pleasure. "Come far?" he inquired.

"Cocklemouth," said Sam with a blank look. "When you've done laughin', what's the joke?"

"Why, there ain't no such place," said the man. "It's just a saying in these parts, that's all."

"Just a wot?" said the bewildered Sam faintly.

"It's just a saying like," said the other, exchanging glances with his friends.

"I don't take you," said the cook. "How can a place be a sayin'?"

"Well, it come through a chap about here named Captain Piggott," said the fisherman, speaking slowly. "He was a wonderful queer old chap, and he got out of his reckoning once, and made—ah, South Amerikey, warn't it, Dan?"

"I believe so," said the old man.

"He thought he'd found a new island," continued the fisherman, "an' he went ashore an' hoisted the Union Jack, and named it arter hisself, Piggott's Bay. Leastways that's the tale his chaps gave out when they come 'ome. Now when anybody's a bit out o' their reckoning we say they're looking for Piggott's Bay. It's just a joke about here."

He began to laugh again, and Sam, noting with regret that he was a big fellow and strong, turned away and followed in the footsteps of the cook, who had already commenced the ascent of the cliff. They paused at the top and looked back; Stone-pen Quay was still laughing.

Moved by a common idea of their personal safety, they struck inland, preferring an additional mile or two to encountering Dick. Conversation was at a discount, and they plodded on sulkily along the dusty road, their lips parched and their legs aching.

They got back to the Seamew at seven o'clock, and greeting Henry, who was in sole charge, with fair words and soothing compliments, persuaded him to make them some tea.

"Where's Dick?" inquired Sam casually as he sat drinking it.

"Ain't seen 'im since dinner," said the boy. "I thought he was with you p'raps."

Sam shook his head, and finishing his tea went on deck with the cook, and gave himself up to all the delights of a quiet sprawl. Fatigued with their exertions, neither of them moved until nine o'clock, and then, with a farewell glance in the direction in which Dick might be expected to come, went below and turned in.

They left the lamp burning, to the great satisfaction of Henry, who was reading, and, as ten o'clock struck somewhere in the town, exchanged anxious glances across the foc'sle concerning Dick's safety. Safe and warm in their bunks, it struck both of them that they had been perhaps a little bit selfish. Half an hour later Henry looked up suddenly as something soft leaped on to the deck above and came pattering towards the foc'sle. The next moment his surprise gave way to indignation, and he raised his voice in tones of expostulation which Mrs. Grundy herself would have envied.

"Dick!" he cried shrilly. "Dick!"

"Shut up!" said Dick fiercely as he flung himself panting on a locker. "O my Lord, I have had a time!"

"I'm surprised at you," said Henry severely, as he dragged some blankets from the bunks and threw them over the exhausted seaman. "Where's your modesty, Dick?"

"If you say another word I'll knock yer ugly little head off!" said Dick wrathfully. "If I hadn't been modest I should have come home by daylight. Oh, I have had a time! I have had a time!"

"Where's your clothes?" inquired Henry.

"How the devil should I know?" snapped the other. "I left 'em on the beach while I went for a swim, and when I comeback they'd gone. I've been sittin' on that damned cold shingle since three o'clock this arternoon, and not a soul come near me! It's the first time I've been lookin' for Cap'n Gething, and it'll be the last."

"Oh, you've been at it, 'ave yer!" said Henry. "I told you you chaps would get in a mess over that."

"You know a damned sight too much for your age!" growled Dick. "There's no call to say anything to Sam and the cook about it, mind."

"Why not?" said Henry.

"Cos I say you're not to," said Dick ferociously. "That's why."

"P'raps they know," said Henry quietly. "Seems to me Sam's listenin' in his sleep."

Dick got up, and going to their bunks inspected the sleep of both his comrades cautiously. Then with a repetition of his caution, strengthened by fearful penalties for disobedience, went to his own bunk and forgot his troubles in sleep. He kept his secret all next day, but his bewilderment when he awoke on Tuesday morning and found the clothes in an untidy brown paper parcel lying on the deck led to its divulgence. He told both Sam and the cook about it, and his opinion of both men went up when he found that they did not treat the matter in the light of a joke, as he had feared. Neither of them even smiled, neither did they extend much sympathy; they listened apathetically, and so soon as he had finished, went straight off to sleep where they sat—a performance which they repeated at every opportunity throughout the whole of the day.

CHAPTER VIII

The Seamew lay at Cocklemouth another three days, in which time Dick, after a twelve-mile walk, learnt all there was to learn about Piggott's Bay. The second outrage was likely to have seriously injured his constitution, but the silver lining of the cloud caught his eye just as he was closing it in sleep, and the tension was removed.

"I've been thinkin', Sam," he said next morning, "that I've been rather selfish over that syndikit business. I ought to 'ave joined it."

"You can please yourself," said Sam.

"But it's better late than never," said Dick, turning to the cook who had joined them. "I'm goin' to put you in the way of findin' Cap'n Gething."

The cook portrayed gratified surprise.

"I know for certain that he's livin' at a place called Piggott's Bay, a little place just up the coast here," continued Dick. "If you two chaps like to walk out this evening and find him you can have two quid apiece and just give me one for myself."

"Oh!" said Sam, and stood thunderstruck at his hardihood.

"But it wouldn't be fair to you, Dick," urged the cook. "We won't take no advantage of you. The five pounds is yours."

"I don't want it," said Dick earnestly. "I want to punish myself for being greedy. If you two 'll just go there and find him I'll take it as a favor."

"Oh, well, we'll go then," said the cook with deceitful joy.

"Dick's 'art's in the right place, cook," observed Sam. "We'd better get away directly arter tea."

"I'd like to shake you by the 'and, Dick," said the cook warmly.

"Me too," said Sam, taking it as the cook relinquished it. "You're a fair brick, Dick, an' no error."

"True blue," said the complimentary cook.

"We'll start directly arter tea, if you'll get us the flag, Dick," said Sam.

"Flag?" said Dick—"flag?"

"Why, yes, the Union Jack," said Sam, looking at him in simple surprise. "It's no use going to Piggott's Bay without a Union Jack? Didn't you know that, Dick? Arter goin' there last night too!"

He stood in an easy attitude waiting for an answer and gazed in clumsy surprise at Dick, as that arch-deceiver stamped his way down below in a fury. He even went so far as to pretend that Dick had gone down for the flag in question, and gingerly putting his head down the scuttle, said that a pair of bathing drawers would do if it was not forthcoming—a piece of pleasantry which he would willingly have withdrawn when the time came for him to meet Dick at dinner.

By the time they reached Northfleet again all interest in the search had practically ceased. For one thing it was an unpleasant thing for grown men to be exposed to the gibes of Henry, and for another, looking at it in the cold clear light of reason, they could but see that there was very little prospect of success. In the cabin pessimism was also to the front with the mate as its mouthpiece.

"It's against all reason," he said, after arguing the matter a little. "You can't expect to find him. Now take my advice, you're doing better with a safe trade between here and Brittlesea—stick to that."

"I won't," said the other doggedly.

"It's hard on 'em," said the mate—"the old men I mean—chevying 'em and hunting 'em about just because they've got gray whiskers and are getting into years. Besides which, some of the crew 'll get into a mess sooner or later."

"Talk as much as you like you won't affect me," retorted the other, who was carrying on the conversation as he was down below washing.

"There you go again," said the mate, "making yourself look nice. What for? Another fellow's girl. Turn it and twist it as much as you please, that's what it comes to."

"When I want your advice," said the skipper, covering his confusion by a vigorous use of the towel, "I'll ask for it."

He finished dressing in silence and went ashore, and after looking about him in a perfunctory fashion, strolled off in the direction of Gravesend. The one gleam of light in his present condition was the regular habits of schools, and as he went along he blessed the strong sense of punctuality which possessed the teaching body at four o'clock.

To-day, however, his congratulations were somewhat premature, for long after the children had come and gone there was no sign of Annis Gething. He walked up and down the road wondering. Half-past four, five. He waited until six o'clock—an object of much interest to sundry ladies who were eyeing him stealthily from their front parlor windows—and was just going at a quarter-past when he saw her coming towards him.

"Back again," she said as she shook hands.

"Just back," said he.

"No news of my father, I suppose?" said Annis. "None, I'm sorry to say," said the skipper. "You're late to-night, aren't you?"

"Rather."

"You look tired," said the skipper with tenderness.

"Well, I'm not," said Annis. "I just stayed and had a cup of tea with Miss Grattan. Mother has gone out, so I didn't hurry."

"Out now?" inquired he.

Miss Gething nodded brightly, and having by this time reached the corner of a road, came to a stop.

"I'm not going in just yet," she said, glancing up the road towards her house. "I'm going for a walk."

"I hope it will be a pleasant one," said Wilson, after a pause, devoted to wondering whether he might venture to offer to accompany her. "Goodbye." He held out his hand.

"Good-bye," said Annis; "if you like to call in and wait to see mother she will be pleased to see you, I'm sure."

"Is there anybody to let me in?" inquired Wilson.

"Mr. Glover is there, I expect," said Annis, looking steadily across the road.

"I—I'll call another time," said the perplexed Wilson, "but I should have thought—"

"Thought what?" said she.

"Nothin'," said he. "I—Are you going for a long walk?"

"Not very far," said she. "Why?"

"I suppose you prefer going alone?"

"I don't mind it," said Annis Gothing; "but you can come if you like."

They turned down the road together, and for some time walked on in silence.

"What was that you were going to say just now?" said Annis, when the silence threatened to become awkward.

"When?" said Wilson.

"When I told you that Mr. Glover was at our house you said you should have thought—" She turned and regarded him with an expression in her eyes which he tried in vain to decipher.

"Well, I should have thought," he said desperately, "that you would have wanted to go there."

"I don't understand you," said Annis coldly. "I think you are rather rude."

"I beg your pardon," said Wilson humbly; "I'm very sorry, very."

There was another long silence, during which they left the road and entered a footpath. It was very narrow, and Annis walked in front.

"I would give anything to find your father," said Wilson earnestly.

"Oh, I wish you could, I wish you could," said Annis, looking at him over her shoulder.

"I suppose Mr. Glover is trying all he can?" said Wilson.

"I want my father!" said Annis with sudden passion—"I want him badly, but I would sooner anybody than Mr. Glover found him!"

"But you are to be married when he is found," said the puzzled Wilson.

"If Mr. Glover finds him," said Annis in a low voice.

"Do you mean to say," said the skipper (in his excitement he caught her by the arm, and she did not release it)—"do you mean to say that you are not going to marry this Glover unless he finds your father?"

"Yes," said Annis, "that is the arrangement. Mother fretted so, and I thought nothing mattered much if we could only find my father. So I promised."

"And I suppose if anybody else finds him?" faltered Wilson, as with a ruthless disregard of growing crops he walked beside her.

"In that case," said Annis, looking at him pleasantly, "I sha'n't marry. Is that what you mean?"

"I didn't mean quite that," said Wilson. "I was going to say—"

"There!" said Annis, stopping suddenly and pointing, "isn't there a fine view of the river from here?"

"Splendid!" said Wilson.

"It is my favorite walk," said Annis.

Wilson made a mental note of it. "Especially when Mr. Glover is at your house," he said foolishly.

"Mr. Glover has been very kind," said Annis gravely. "He has been very good to my mother, and he has gone to a great deal of trouble in his search for my father."

"Well, I hope he doesn't find him," said Wilson. Annis turned and regarded him fixedly. "That is very kind of you," she said with severity.

"I want to find him myself," said Wilson, closely watching the river; "and you know why."

"I must get back," said Annis, without contesting the statement.

Wilson felt his courage oozing, and tried to hint at what he dared not say. "I should like you to treat me the same as you do Mr. Glover," he said nervously.

"I'll do that with pleasure," said Annis promptly. In spite of herself her lips quivered and her eyes danced.

"I've loved you ever since the first time I saw you!" said Wilson with sudden vehemence.

Utterly unprepared for this direct attack, Miss Gething had no weapon to meet it. The tables were turned, and reddening with confusion, she looked away and made no reply.

"I've spent days walking up and down the road the school is in because you were there," continued Wilson. "I've wondered sometimes that the school children didn't notice it."

Miss Gething turned to him a cheek which was of the richest carmine, "If it's any pleasure to you to know it, they did," she said viciously. "I taught one small infant the blessing of silence by keeping her in three afternoons."

"I can't help it," said Wilson. "You'll have to keep the whole school in before I get over my fondness for that road. What did she say?"

"Suppose we get back," said Annis coldly, and turning, walked silently beside him. Neither spoke until they reached the lane again, and then Wilson stopped and met her gaze full and fair. Miss Gething, after a brave trial, abandoned the contest and lowered her eyes.

"Will you serve us both alike?" said Wilson in a low voice.

"No," said Annis. She looked up at him shyly and smiled. A light broke in upon him, and seizing her hand he drew her towards him.

"No," said Annis, drawing back sharply; "it wouldn't be right."

Afraid he had gone too far, Wilson's cowardice got the better hand again. "What wouldn't?" he asked, with an awkward attempt at innocence. A tiny but ominous sparkle in Miss Gething's eye showed her opinion of this unfairness.

"I beg your pardon," he said humbly.

"What for?" asked Miss Gething innocently in her turn.

Soon tired of devious paths, in which he lost himself, Wilson tried a direct one again. "For trying to kiss you and then pretending I didn't know what you meant when you refused," he said bluntly.

"Captain Wilson!" said Miss Gething breathlessly, "I—I don't know what you mean."

"Yes you do," said Wilson calmly.

The sparkle came in Miss Gething's eye again, then she bit her lip and turned her head away miserably realizing her inability to treat this transgressor with the severity that he deserved.

"This is the first time you have ever said things of this sort to a girl, I should think," she said at last.

"Yes," said Wilson simply.

"You want practice," said Miss Gething scornfully.

"That's just what I do want," said Wilson eagerly.

He was moving towards her again, but she checked him with a look.

"But not with a girl who is half engaged to another man," she said, regarding him with soft eyes; "it isn't right."

"Does he know how it is?" inquired Wilson, referring, of course, to the absent Glover.

Miss Gething nodded.

"I think it's quite right and proper, then," said Wilson.

"I don't," said Annis, holding out her hand. "I'll say good-bye," she said steadily. "I won't see you again until my father is found. If Mr. Glover finds him I won't see you at all. Good-bye."

The skipper took her hand, and marvelling at his pluck, drew her, resisting slightly, towards him again. Then he bent his head, and, with the assistance of Miss Gething, kissed the brim of her hat. Then she broke from him and ran lightly up the lane, pausing at the end to stop and wave her hand ere she disappeared. The skipper waved his in return, and glancing boldly at a horse which had witnessed all the proceedings from over the hedge, walked back to Northfleet to urge his dispirited crew to still further efforts.

CHAPTER IX

To the skipper's surprise and disapproval Annis kept her word. To be sure she could not prevent him meeting her in the road when the schooner was at Northfleet, his attitude when she tried to, being one of wilful and deliberate defiance. She met this disobedience adeptly by taking a pupil home with her, and when even this was not sufficient added to the number. The day on which she appeared in the road with four small damsels was the last day the skipper accompanied her. He could only walk in front or behind; the conversation was severely technical, and the expression on the small girls' faces precocious in the extreme.

The search went on all the summer, the crew of the Seamew causing much comment at the various ports by walking about as though they had lost something. They all got to wear a bereaved appearance after a time, which, in the case of the cook—who had risked some capital in the affair—was gradually converted to one of resignation.

At the beginning of September they found themselves at Ironbridge, a small town on the East Coast, situated on the river Lebben. As usual, the skipper's inquiries revealed nothing. Ironbridge was a small place, with absolutely nothing to conceal; but it was a fine day, and Henry, who disliked extremely the task of assisting to work out the cargo, obtained permission to go ashore to purchase a few small things for the cook and look round.

He strolled along blithely, casting a glance over his shoulders at the dusty cloud which hung over the Seamew as he went. It was virgin soil to him, and he thirsted for adventure.

The town contained but few objects of interest. Before the advent of railways it had been a thriving port with a considerable trade; now its streets were sleepy and its wharves deserted. Besides the Seamew the only other craft in the river was a tiny sloop, the cargo of which two men were unloading by means of a basket and pulley and a hand truck.

The quietude told upon Henry, who, after a modest half-pint, lit his pipe and sauntered along the narrow High Street with his hands in his pockets. A short walk brought him to the white hurdles of the desolate market-place. Here the town as a town ended and gave place to a few large houses standing in their own grounds.

"Well, give me London," said Henry to himself as he paused at a high brick wall and looked at the fruit trees beyond. "Why, the place seems dead!"

He scrambled up on to the wall, and, perched on the top, whistled softly. The grown-up flavor of half-pints had not entirely eradicated a youthful partiality for apples. He was hidden from the house by the trees, and almost involuntarily he dropped down on the other side of the wall and began to fill his pockets with the fruit.

Things were so quiet that he became venturesome, and, imitating the stealthy movement of the Red Indian, whom he loved, so far as six or seven pounds of apples would allow him, made his way to a large summer-house and peeped in. It was empty, except for a table and a couple of rough benches, and after another careful look round, he entered, and seating himself on the bench, tried an apple.

He was roused to a sense of the danger of his position by footsteps on the path outside, which, coming nearer and nearer, were evidently aimed at the summer-house. With a silence and celerity of which any brave would have been proud, he got under the table.

"There you are, you naughty little girl," said a woman's voice. "You will not come out until you know your rivers perfectly."

Somebody was pushed into the summer-house, the door slammed behind, and a key turned in the lock. The footsteps retreated again, and the embarrassed brave realized that he was in a cruelly false position, his very life, so to speak, depending on the strength a small girl's scream.

"I don't care!" said a dogged voice. "Bother your rivers! bother your rivers! bother your rivers!"

The owner of the voice sat on the table and hummed fiercely. In the stress of mental anguish caused by his position, Henry made a miscalculation, and in turning bumped the table heavily with his head.

"Ough!" said the small girl breathlessly.

"Don't be frightened," said Henry, popping up humbly; "I won't hurt you."

"Hoo!" said the small girl in a flutter; "a boy!"

Henry rose and seated himself respectfully, coughing confusedly, as he saw the small girl's gaze riveted on his pockets.

"What have you got in your pockets?" she asked.

"Apples," said Henry softly. "I bought 'em in the town."

The small girl extended her hand, and accepting a couple, inspected them carefully.

"You're a bad, wicked boy!" she said seriously as she bit into one. "You'll get it when Miss Dimchurch comes!"

"Who's Miss Dimchurch?" inquired Henry with pardonable curiosity.

"Schoolmistress," said the small girl.

"Is this a school?" said Henry.

The small girl, her mouth full of apple, nodded.

"Any men here?" inquired Henry with an assumed carelessness.

The small girl shook her head.

"You're the only boy I've ever seen here," she said gleefully. "You'll get it when Miss Dimchurch comes!"

His mind relieved of a great fear, Henry leaned back and smiled confidently.

"I'm not afraid of the old girl," he said quietly, as he pulled out his pipe and filled it.

The small girl's eyes glistened with admiration.

"I wish I was a boy," she said plaintively, "then I shouldn't mind her. Are you a sailor-boy?"

"Sailor," corrected Henry; "yes."

"I like sailors," said the small girl amicably. "You may have a bite of my apple if you like."

"Never mind, thanks," said Henry hastily; "I've got a clean one here."

The small girl drew herself up and eyed him haughtily, but finding that he was not looking at her resumed her apple.

"What's your name?" she asked.

"'Enery Hatkins," replied the youth, as he remembered sundry cautions about the letter h he had received at school. "What's yours?"

"Gertrude Ursula Florence Harcourt," said the small girl, sitting up straighter to say it. "I don't like the name of Atkins."

"Don't you?" said Henry, trying not to show resentment. "I don't like Gertrude, or Ursula, or Florence, and Harcourt's the worst of all."

Miss Harcourt drew off three or four inches and drummed with the tips of her fingers on the table. "I don't care what you like," she said humming.

"I like Gerty," said Henry with the air of a connoisseur, as he looked at the small flushed face. "I think Gerty's very pretty."

"That's what they always call me," said Miss Harcourt carelessly. "Does your ship go right out to sea?"

"Yes," said the boy. They had been blown out to sea once, and he salved his conscience with that.

"And how many times," said Gertrude Ursula Florence Harcourt, getting nearer to him again, "have you had fights with pirates?"

She left absolutely no loophole. If she had asked him whether he had ever fought pirates he would have said "No," though that would have been hard with her little excitable face turned towards his and the dark blue eyes dancing with interest.

"I forget whether it was six or seven," said Henry Atkins. "I think it was only six."

"Tell us all about them," said Miss Harcourt, shifting with excitement.

Henry took a bite of his apple and started, thankful that a taste for reading of a thrilling description had furnished him with material. He fought ships in a way which even admirals had never thought of, and certainly not the pirates, who were invariably discomfited by the ingenious means by which he enabled virtue to triumph over sin. Miss Harcourt held her breath with pleasurable terror, and tightened or relaxed the grip of her small and not too clean fingers on his arm as the narrative proceeded.

"But you never killed a man yourself," said she, when he had finished. There was an inflection, just a slight inflection, of voice, which Henry thought undeserved after the trouble he had taken.

"I can't exactly say," he replied shortly. "You see in the heat"—he got it right that time—"in the heat of an engagement you can't be sure."

"Of course you can't," said Miss Harcourt, repenting of her unreasonableness. "You are brave!" Henry blushed.

"Are you an officer?" inquired Miss Harcourt.

"Not quite," said Henry, wishing somehow that he was.

"If you make haste and become an officer I'll marry you when I grow up," said Miss Harcourt, smiling on him kindly. "That is if you like, of course."

"I should like it very much," said Henry wistfully, "I didn't mean it when I said I didn't like your names just now."

"You shouldn't have told stories, then," said Miss Harcourt severely, but not unkindly; "I can't bear storytellers."

The conscience-stricken Henry groaned inwardly, but, reflecting there was plenty of time to confess before the marriage, brightened up again. The "Rivers of Europe" had fallen beneath the table, and were entirely forgotten until the sounds of many feet and many voices in the garden recalled them to a sense of their position.

"Play-time," said the small girl, picking up her book and skipping to the farthest seat possible from Henry. "Thames, Seine, Danube, Rhine."

A strong, firm step stopped outside the door, and a key turned in the lock. The door was thrown open, and Miss Dimchurch peeping in, drew back with a cry of surprise. Behind her some thirty small girls, who saw her surprise, but not the reason for it, waited eagerly for light.

"Miss Harcourt!" said the principal in an awful voice.

"Yes, ma'am," said Miss Harcourt looking up, with her finger in the book to keep the place.

"How dare you stay in here with this person?" demanded the principal.

"It wasn't my fault," said Miss Harcourt, working up a whimper. "You locked me in. He was here when I came."

"Why didn't you call after me?" demanded Miss Dimchurch.

"I didn't know he was here; he was under the table," said Miss Harcourt.

Miss Dimchurch turned and bestowed a terrible glance upon Henry, who, with his forgotten pipe in his hand, looked uneasily up to see whether he could push past her. Miss Harcourt, holding her breath, gazed at the destroyer of pirates, and waited confidently for something extraordinary to happen.

"He's been stealing my apples!" said Miss Dimchurch tragically. "Where's the gymnasium mistress?"

The gymnasium mistress, a tall pretty girl, was just behind her.

"Remove that horrid boy, Miss O'Brien," said the principal.

"Don't worry," said Henry, trying to speak calmly; "I'll go. Stand away here. I don't want to be hard on wimmin."

"Take him out," commanded the mistress.

Miss O'Brien, pleased at this opportunity of displaying her powers, entered, and squaring her shoulders, stood over the intruder in much the same way that Henry had seen barmen stand over Sam.

"Look here, now," he said, turning pale; "you drop it. I don't want to hurt you."

He placed his pipe in his pocket, and rose to his feet as the gymnasium mistress caught him in her strong slender arms and raised him from the ground. Her grip was like steel, and a babel of admiring young voices broke upon his horrified ears as his captor marched easily with him down the garden, their progress marked by apples, which rolled out of his pockets and bounded along the ground.

"I shall kick you," whispered Henry fiercely—ignoring the fact that both legs were jammed together—as he caught sight of the pale, bewildered little face of Gertrude U. F. Harcourt.

"Kick away," said Miss O'Brien sweetly, and using him as a dumb-bell, threw in a gratuitous gymnastic display for the edification of her pupils.

"If you come here again, you naughty little boy," said Miss Dimchurch, who was heading the procession behind, "I shall give you to a policeman. Open the gate, girls!"

The gate was open, and Henry, half dead with shame, was thrust into the road in full view of the cook, who had been sent out in search of him.

"Wot, 'Enery?" said the cook in unbelieving accents as he staggered back, aghast at the spectacle— "wotever 'ave you been a-doin' of?"

"He's been stealing my apples!" said Miss Dimchurch sternly. "If I catch him here again I shall cane him!"

"Quite right, ma'am! I hope he hasn't hurt anybody," said the cook, unable to realize fully the discomfiture of the youth.

Miss Dimchurch slammed the gate and left the couple standing in the road. The cook turned and led the way down to the town again, accompanied by the crestfallen Henry.

"'Ave a apple, cook?" said the latter, proffering one; "I saved a beauty a-purpose for you."

"No, thanks," said the cook.

"It won't bite you," said Henry shortly.

"No, and I won't bite it either," replied the cook.

They continued their way in silence, until at the market-place Henry paused in front of the "Farmer's Arms."

"Come in and 'ave a pint, old chap," he said cordially.

"No, thankee," said the cook again. "It's no use, Enery, you don't git over me in that way."

"Wot d'ye mean?" blustered the youth.

"You know," said the other darkly.

"No, I don't," said Henry.

"Well, I wouldn't miss tellin' the other chaps, no, not for six pints," said the cook cheerfully. "You're a deep un, 'Enery, but so am I."

"Glad you told me," said the out-generalled youth "Nobody'd think so to look at your silly, fat face."

The cook smiled indulgently, and, going aboard, left his youthful charge to give the best explanation he could of his absence to the skipper—an explanation which was marred for him by the childish behavior of the cook at the other end of the ship, who taking the part of Miss O'Brien for himself, gave that of Henry to a cork fender, which, when it became obstreperous—as it frequently did on the slightest provocation—he slapped vigorously, giving sundry falsetto howls, which he fondly imagined were in good imitation of Henry. After three encores the skipper stepped forward for enlightenment, returning to the mate with a grin so aggravating that the sensitive Henry was near to receiving a thrashing for insubordination of the most impertinent nature.

To the skipper's surprise and disapproval Annis kept her word. To be sure she could not prevent him meeting her in the road when the schooner was at Northfleet, his attitude when she tried to, being one of wilful and deliberate defiance. She met this disobedience adeptly by taking a pupil home with her, and when even this was not sufficient added to the number. The day on which she appeared in the road with four small damsels was the last day the skipper accompanied her. He could only walk in front or behind; the conversation was severely technical, and the expression on the small girls' faces precocious in the extreme.

The search went on all the summer, the crew of the Seamew causing much comment at the various ports by walking about as though they had lost something. They all got to wear a bereaved appearance after a time, which, in the case of the cook—who had risked some capital in the affair— was gradually converted to one of resignation.

At the beginning of September they found themselves at Ironbridge, a small town on the East Coast, situated on the river Lebben. As usual, the skipper's inquiries revealed nothing. Ironbridge was a small place, with absolutely nothing to conceal; but it was a fine day, and Henry, who disliked extremely the task of assisting to work out the cargo, obtained permission to go ashore to purchase a few small things for the cook and look round.

He strolled along blithely, casting a glance over his shoulders at the dusty cloud which hung over the Seamew as he went. It was virgin soil to him, and he thirsted for adventure.

The town contained but few objects of interest. Before the advent of railways it had been a thriving port with a considerable trade; now its streets were sleepy and its wharves deserted. Besides the Seamew the only other craft in the river was a tiny sloop, the cargo of which two men were unloading by means of a basket and pulley and a hand truck.

The quietude told upon Henry, who, after a modest half-pint, lit his pipe and sauntered along the narrow High Street with his hands in his pockets. A short walk brought him to the white hurdles of the desolate market-place. Here the town as a town ended and gave place to a few large houses standing in their own grounds.

"Well, give me London," said Henry to himself as he paused at a high brick wall and looked at the fruit trees beyond. "Why, the place seems dead!"

He scrambled up on to the wall, and, perched on the top, whistled softly. The grown-up flavor of half-pints had not entirely eradicated a youthful partiality for apples. He was hidden from the house by the trees, and almost involuntarily he dropped down on the other side of the wall and began to fill his pockets with the fruit.

Things were so quiet that he became venturesome, and, imitating the stealthy movement of the Red Indian, whom he loved, so far as six or seven pounds of apples would allow him, made his way to a large summer-house and peeped in. It was empty, except for a table and a couple of rough benches, and after another careful look round, he entered, and seating himself on the bench, tried an apple.

He was roused to a sense of the danger of his position by footsteps on the path outside, which, coming nearer and nearer, were evidently aimed at the summer-house. With a silence and celerity of which any brave would have been proud, he got under the table.

"There you are, you naughty little girl," said a woman's voice. "You will not come out until you know your rivers perfectly."

Somebody was pushed into the summer-house, the door slammed behind, and a key turned in the lock. The footsteps retreated again, and the embarrassed brave realized that he was in a cruelly false position, his very life, so to speak, depending on the strength a small girl's scream.

"I don't care!" said a dogged voice. "Bother your rivers! bother your rivers! bother your rivers!"

The owner of the voice sat on the table and hummed fiercely. In the stress of mental anguish caused by his position, Henry made a miscalculation, and in turning bumped the table heavily with his head.

"Ough!" said the small girl breathlessly.

"Don't be frightened," said Henry, popping up humbly; "I won't hurt you."

"Hoo!" said the small girl in a flutter; "a boy!"

Henry rose and seated himself respectfully, coughing confusedly, as he saw the small girl's gaze riveted on his pockets.

"What have you got in your pockets?" she asked.

"Apples," said Henry softly. "I bought 'em in the town."

The small girl extended her hand, and accepting a couple, inspected them carefully.

"You're a bad, wicked boy!" she said seriously as she bit into one. "You'll get it when Miss Dimchurch comes!"

"Who's Miss Dimchurch?" inquired Henry with pardonable curiosity.

"Schoolmistress," said the small girl.

"Is this a school?" said Henry.

The small girl, her mouth full of apple, nodded.

"Any men here?" inquired Henry with an assumed carelessness.

The small girl shook her head.

"You're the only boy I've ever seen here," she said gleefully. "You'll get it when Miss Dimchurch comes!"

His mind relieved of a great fear, Henry leaned back and smiled confidently.

"I'm not afraid of the old girl," he said quietly, as he pulled out his pipe and filled it.

The small girl's eyes glistened with admiration.

"I wish I was a boy," she said plaintively, "then I shouldn't mind her. Are you a sailor-boy?"

"Sailor," corrected Henry; "yes."

"I like sailors," said the small girl amicably. "You may have a bite of my apple if you like."

"Never mind, thanks," said Henry hastily; "I've got a clean one here."

The small girl drew herself up and eyed him haughtily, but finding that he was not looking at her resumed her apple.

"What's your name?" she asked.

"'Enery Hatkins," replied the youth, as he remembered sundry cautions about the letter h he had received at school. "What's yours?"

"Gertrude Ursula Florence Harcourt," said the small girl, sitting up straighter to say it. "I don't like the name of Atkins."

"Don't you?" said Henry, trying not to show resentment. "I don't like Gertrude, or Ursula, or Florence, and Harcourt's the worst of all."

Miss Harcourt drew off three or four inches and drummed with the tips of her fingers on the table. "I don't care what you like," she said humming.

"I like Gerty," said Henry with the air of a connoisseur, as he looked at the small flushed face. "I think Gerty's very pretty."

"That's what they always call me," said Miss Harcourt carelessly. "Does your ship go right out to sea?"

"Yes," said the boy. They had been blown out to sea once, and he salved his conscience with that.

"And how many times," said Gertrude Ursula Florence Harcourt, getting nearer to him again, "have you had fights with pirates?"

She left absolutely no loophole. If she had asked him whether he had ever fought pirates he would have said "No," though that would have been hard with her little excitable face turned towards his and the dark blue eyes dancing with interest.

"I forget whether it was six or seven," said Henry Atkins. "I think it was only six."

"Tell us all about them," said Miss Harcourt, shifting with excitement.

Henry took a bite of his apple and started, thankful that a taste for reading of a thrilling description had furnished him with material. He fought ships in a way which even admirals had never thought of, and certainly not the pirates, who were invariably discomfited by the ingenious means by which he enabled virtue to triumph over sin. Miss Harcourt held her breath with pleasurable terror, and tightened or relaxed the grip of her small and not too clean fingers on his arm as the narrative proceeded.

"But you never killed a man yourself," said she, when he had finished. There was an inflection, just a slight inflection, of voice, which Henry thought undeserved after the trouble he had taken.

"I can't exactly say," he replied shortly. "You see in the heat"—he got it right that time—"in the heat of an engagement you can't be sure."

"Of course you can't," said Miss Harcourt, repenting of her unreasonableness. "You are brave!" Henry blushed.

"Are you an officer?" inquired Miss Harcourt.

"Not quite," said Henry, wishing somehow that he was.

"If you make haste and become an officer I'll marry you when I grow up," said Miss Harcourt, smiling on him kindly. "That is if you like, of course."

"I should like it very much," said Henry wistfully, "I didn't mean it when I said I didn't like your names just now."

"You shouldn't have told stories, then," said Miss Harcourt severely, but not unkindly; "I can't bear storytellers."

The conscience-stricken Henry groaned inwardly, but, reflecting there was plenty of time to confess before the marriage, brightened up again. The "Rivers of Europe" had fallen beneath the table, and were entirely forgotten until the sounds of many feet and many voices in the garden recalled them to a sense of their position.

"Play-time," said the small girl, picking up her book and skipping to the farthest seat possible from Henry. "Thames, Seine, Danube, Rhine."

A strong, firm step stopped outside the door, and a key turned in the lock. The door was thrown open, and Miss Dimchurch peeping in, drew back with a cry of surprise. Behind her some thirty small girls, who saw her surprise, but not the reason for it, waited eagerly for light.

"Miss Harcourt!" said the principal in an awful voice.

"Yes, ma'am," said Miss Harcourt looking up, with her finger in the book to keep the place.

"How dare you stay in here with this person?" demanded the principal.

"It wasn't my fault," said Miss Harcourt, working up a whimper. "You locked me in. He was here when I came."

"Why didn't you call after me?" demanded Miss Dimchurch.

"I didn't know he was here; he was under the table," said Miss Harcourt.

Miss Dimchurch turned and bestowed a terrible glance upon Henry, who, with his forgotten pipe in his hand, looked uneasily up to see whether he could push past her. Miss Harcourt, holding her breath, gazed at the destroyer of pirates, and waited confidently for something extraordinary to happen.

"He's been stealing my apples!" said Miss Dimchurch tragically. "Where's the gymnasium mistress?"

The gymnasium mistress, a tall pretty girl, was just behind her.

"Remove that horrid boy, Miss O'Brien," said the principal.

"Don't worry," said Henry, trying to speak calmly; "I'll go. Stand away here. I don't want to be hard on wimmin."

"Take him out," commanded the mistress.

Miss O'Brien, pleased at this opportunity of displaying her powers, entered, and squaring her shoulders, stood over the intruder in much the same way that Henry had seen barmen stand over Sam.

"Look here, now," he said, turning pale; "you drop it. I don't want to hurt you."

He placed his pipe in his pocket, and rose to his feet as the gymnasium mistress caught him in her strong slender arms and raised him from the ground. Her grip was like steel, and a babel of admiring young voices broke upon his horrified ears as his captor marched easily with him down the garden, their progress marked by apples, which rolled out of his pockets and bounded along the ground.

"I shall kick you," whispered Henry fiercely—ignoring the fact that both legs were jammed together—as he caught sight of the pale, bewildered little face of Gertrude U. F. Harcourt.

"Kick away," said Miss O'Brien sweetly, and using him as a dumb-bell, threw in a gratuitous gymnastic display for the edification of her pupils.

"If you come here again, you naughty little boy," said Miss Dimchurch, who was heading the procession behind, "I shall give you to a policeman. Open the gate, girls!"

The gate was open, and Henry, half dead with shame, was thrust into the road in full view of the cook, who had been sent out in search of him.

"Wot, 'Enery?" said the cook in unbelieving accents as he staggered back, aghast at the spectacle— "wotever 'ave you been a-doin' of?"

"He's been stealing my apples!" said Miss Dimchurch sternly. "If I catch him here again I shall cane him!"

"Quite right, ma'am! I hope he hasn't hurt anybody," said the cook, unable to realize fully the discomfiture of the youth.

Miss Dimchurch slammed the gate and left the couple standing in the road. The cook turned and led the way down to the town again, accompanied by the crestfallen Henry.

"'Ave a apple, cook?" said the latter, proffering one; "I saved a beauty a-purpose for you."

"No, thanks," said the cook.

"It won't bite you," said Henry shortly.

"No, and I won't bite it either," replied the cook.

They continued their way in silence, until at the market-place Henry paused in front of the "Farmer's Arms."

"Come in and 'ave a pint, old chap," he said cordially.

"No, thankee," said the cook again. "It's no use, Enery, you don't git over me in that way."

"Wot d'ye mean?" blustered the youth.

"You know," said the other darkly.

"No, I don't," said Henry.

"Well, I wouldn't miss tellin' the other chaps, no, not for six pints," said the cook cheerfully. "You're a deep un, 'Enery, but so am I."

"Glad you told me," said the out-generalled youth "Nobody'd think so to look at your silly, fat face."

The cook smiled indulgently, and, going aboard, left his youthful charge to give the best explanation he could of his absence to the skipper—an explanation which was marred for him by the childish behavior of the cook at the other end of the ship, who taking the part of Miss O'Brien for himself, gave that of Henry to a cork fender, which, when it became obstreperous—as it frequently did on the slightest provocation—he slapped vigorously, giving sundry falsetto howls, which he fondly imagined were in good imitation of Henry. After three encores the skipper stepped forward for enlightenment, returning to the mate with a grin so aggravating that the sensitive Henry was near to receiving a thrashing for insubordination of the most impertinent nature.

CHAPTER X

From Ironbridge, two days later, they sailed with a general cargo for Stourwich, the Seamew picking her way carefully down the river by moonlight, followed at an ever-increasing distance by a cork fender of abandoned aspect.

A great change had come over Henry, and an attitude of proud reserve had taken the place of the careless banter with which he usually regaled the crew. He married Miss O'Brien in imagination to a strong man of villainous temper and despotic ideas, while the explanations he made to Miss Harcourt were too ingenious and involved to be confined in the space of a single chapter. To these daydreams, idle though he knew they were, he turned as a welcome relief from the coarse vulgarity of the crew.

Sympathy had widened his ideas, and he now felt a tender but mournful interest in the skipper's affairs. He read aloud to himself at every opportunity, and aspirated his h's until he made his throat ache. His aspirations also extended to his conversation, until at last the mate told him plainly "that if he blew in his face again he'd get his ears boxed."

They passed the breakwater and dropped anchor in the harbor of Stourwich just as the rising sun was glowing red on the steeple of the town church. The narrow, fishy little streets leading from the quay were deserted, except for one lane, down which sleepy passengers were coming in twos and threes to catch the boat, which was chafing and grinding against the timbers of the jetty and pouring from its twin-funnels dense volumes of smoke to take the sting out of the morning air.

Little by little as the Seamew who was not quite certain as to her berth, rode at anchor, the town came to life again. Men of marine appearance, in baggy trousers and tight jerseys, came slowly on to the quay and stared meditatively at the water or shouted vehemently at other men, who had got into small boats to bale them out with rusty cans. From some of these loungers, after much shouting and contradictory information, the Seamew, discovered her destination and was soon fast alongside.

The cargo—a very small one—was out by three o'clock that afternoon, and the crew, having replaced the hatches and cleaned up, went ashore together, after extending an invitation to Henry—which was coldly declined—to go with them.

The skipper was already ashore, and the boy, after enduring for some time the witticisms of the mate, on the subject of apples, went too.

For some time he wandered aimlessly about the town, with his hands in his pockets. The season was drawing to an end, but a few holiday-makers were lounging about on the parade, or venturing carefully along the dreary breakwater to get the full benefit of the sea air. Idly watching these and other objects of interest on the sea-shore, the boy drifted on until he found himself at the adjoining watering-place of Overcourt.

The parade ended in two flights of steps, one of which led to the sands and the other to the road and the cliffs above. For people who cared for neither, thoughtful local authorities had placed a long seat, and on this Henry placed himself and sat for some time, regarding with the lenity of age the erratic sports of the children below. He had sat there for some time when he became idly interested in the movements of an old man walking along the sands to the steps. Arrived at the foot he disappeared from sight, then a huge hand gripped the handrail, and a peaked cloth cap was revealed to the suddenly interested Henry, for the face of the old man was the face of the well-thumbed photograph in the foc'sle.

Unconscious of the wild excitement in the breast of the small boy on the seat, the old man paused to take breath for the next flight.

"Have you—got such a thing as a—as a match—about you?" said Henry, trying to speak calmly, but failing.

"You're over-young to smoke," said the old man, turning round and regarding him.

At any other time, with any other person, Henry's retort to this would have been rude, but the momentous events which depended on his civility restrained him.

"I find it soothing," he said with much gravity, "if I get overworked or worried."

The old man regarded him with unfeigned astonishment, a grim smile lurking at the corners of his well-hidden mouth.

"If you were my boy," he said shortly, as he put his forefinger and thumb into his waistcoat pocket and extracted a time-stained lucifer, "do you know what I'd do to you?"

"Stop me smoking?" hazarded Henry cheerfully.

"I would that," said the other, turning to go.

"How old were you when you started smoking?" asked the boy.

"About your age, I expect," said the old man slowly; "but I was a much bigger chap than you are. A stunted little chap like you ought not to smoke."

Henry smiled wanly, and began to think that the five pounds would be well earned.

"Will you have a pipe?" he said, proffering a gaudy pouch.

"Confound you!" said the old man, flashing into sudden weak anger. "When I want your tobacco I'll ask you for it."

"No offence," said the boy hastily, "no offence. It's some I bought cheap, and our chaps said I'd been 'ad. I only wanted to see what you thought of it."

The old man hesitated a moment, and then taking the seat beside him, accepted the proffered pouch and smelt the contents critically. Then he drew a small black clay from his pocket and slowly filled it.

"Smokes all right," he said after a few puffs. He leaned back, and half closing his eyes, smoked with the enjoyment of an old smoker to whom a pipe is a somewhat rare luxury, while Henry regarded his shabby clothes and much-patched boots with great interest.

"Stranger here?" inquired the old man amiably.

"Schooner Seamew down in the harbor," said Henry, indicating the distant town of Stourwich with a wave of his hand.

"Ay, ay," said the old man, and smoked in silence.

"Got to stay here for a few days," said Henry, watching him out of the tail of his eye; "then back."

"London?" suggested the other.

"Northfleet," said Henry carelessly, "that's where we came from."

The old man's face twitched ever so slightly, and he blew out a cloud of smoke.

"Do you live there?" he inquired.

"Wapping," said Henry; "but I know Northfleet very well—Gravesend too. Ever been there?"

"Never," said the old man emphatically; "never."

"Rather a nice place, I think," said Henry; "I like it better than Wapping. We've sailed from there a year now. Our skipper is fond of it too. He's rather sweet on a girl who's teacher in a school there."

"What school?" asked the old man.

The boy gave a slight laugh. "Well, it's no good telling you if you don't know the place," he said easily; "it's a girls' school."

"I used to know a man that lived there," said the other, speaking slowly and carefully. "What's her name?"

"I forget," said the boy, yawning.

Conversation flagged, and the two sat idly watching the last of the children as they toiled slowly towards home from the sands. The sun had set and the air was getting chilly.

"I'll be getting home," said the old man. "Goodnight, my lad."

"Good-night to you," said the well-mannered Henry.

He watched the old man's still strong figure as it passed slowly up the steps, and allowing him to get some little distance start, cautiously followed. He followed him up the steps and along the cliff, the figure in front never halting until it reached a small court at the back of a livery stable; then, heedless of the small shadow, now very close behind, it pushed open the door of a dirty little house and entered. The shadow crept up and paused irresolute, and then, after a careful survey of the place, stole silently and swiftly away.

The shadow, choosing the road because it was quicker, now danced back to Stourwich, and jumping lightly on to the schooner, came behind the cook and thumped him heavily on the back. Before the cook could seize him he had passed on to Sam, and embracing as much of that gentleman's waist as possible, vainly besought him to dance.

"'E's off 'is 'ead," said Sam, shaking himself free and regarding him unfavorably. "What's wrong, kiddy?"

"Nothing," said Henry jubilantly; "everything's right."

"More happles?" said the cook with a nasty sneer.

"No, it ain't apples," said Henry hotly; "you never get more than one idea at a time into that 'ead of yours. Where's the skipper? I've got something important to tell 'im—something that'll make 'im dance."

"Wot is it?" said the cook and Sam together turning pale.

"Now don't get excited," said Henry, holding up his hand warningly; "it's bad for you, Sam, because you're too fat, and it's bad for cookie because 'is 'ead's weak. You'll know all in good time."

He walked aft, leaving them to confer uneasily as to the cause of his jubilant condition, and hastily descending the companion ladder, burst noisily into the cabin and surveyed the skipper and mate with a smile, which he intended should be full of information. Both looked up in surprise, and the skipper, who was in a very bad temper, half rose from his seat.

"Where've you been, you young rascal?" he asked, eyeing him sternly.

"Looking around," said Henry, still smiling as he thought of the change in the skipper's manner when he should disclose his information.

"This is the second time you've taken yourself off," roared the other angrily. "I've half a mind to give you the soundest thrashing you ever had in your life."

"All right," said Henry, somewhat taken aback. "When—"

"Don't answer me, you idle young rascal!" said the skipper sternly; "get to bed."

"I want to—" began Henry, chilled by this order.

"Get to bed," repeated the skipper, rising.

"Bed?" said Henry, as his face hardened; "bed at seven o'clock?"

"I'll punish you somehow," said the skipper, looking from him to the cook who had just descended. "Cook!"

"Yes, sir," said the cook briskly.

"Put that boy to bed," said the other, "and see he goes now."

"A' right, sir," said the grinning cook. "Come along, 'Enery."

With a pale face and a haughty mien, which under other circumstances might have been extremely impressive, Henry, after an entreating glance at the skipper, followed him up the steps.

"'E's got to go to bed," said the cook to Sam and Dick, who were standing together. "'E's been naughty."

"Who said so?" asked Sam eagerly.

"Skipper," replied the cook. "'E told me we wos to put him to bed ourselves."

"You needn't trouble," said Henry stiffly; "I'll go all right."

"It's no trouble," said Sam oilily.

"It's a pleasure," said Dick truthfully.

Arrived at the scuttle, Henry halted, and with an assumption of ease he was far from feeling, yawned, and looked round at the night.

"Go to bed," said Sam reprovingly, and seizing him in his stout arms passed him below to the cook, feet first, as the cook discovered to his cost.

"'E ought to be bathed first," said Sam, assuming the direction of affairs; "and it's Monday night, and 'e ought to have a clean nightgown on."

"Is 'is little bed made?" inquired the cook anxiously.

"'Is little bed's just proper," said Dick, patting it.

"We won't bathe him to-night," said Sam, as he tied a towel apron-wise round his waist; "it 'ud be too long a job. Now, 'Enery, come on to my lap."

Aided by willing arms, he took the youth on to his knee, and despite his frantic struggles, began to prepare him for his slumbers. At the pressing request of the cook he removed the victim's boots first, and, as Dick said, it was surprising what a difference it made. Then having washed the boy's face with soap and flannel, he lifted him into his berth, grinning respectfully up at the face of the mate as it peered down from the scuttle with keen enjoyment of the scene.

"Is the boy asleep?" he inquired aggravatingly, as Henry's arms and legs shot out of the berth in mad attempts to reach his tormentors.

"Sleeping like a little hangel, sir!" said Sam respectfully. "Would you like to come down and see he's all right, sir?"

"Bless him!" said the grinning mate.

He went off, and Henry, making the best of a bad job, closed his eyes and refused to be drawn into replying to the jests of the men. Ever since he had been on the schooner he had been free from punishment of all kinds by the strict order of the skipper—a situation of which he had taken the fullest advantage. Now his power was shaken, and he lay grinding his teeth as he thought of the indignity to which he had been subjected.

CHAPTER XI

He resolved that he would keep his discovery to himself. It was an expensive luxury, but he determined to indulge in it, and months or years later perhaps he would allow the skipper to learn what he had lost by his overbearing brutality. Somewhat soothed by this idea, he fell asleep.

His determination, which was strong when he arose, weakened somewhat as the morning wore on. The skipper, who had thought no more of the matter after giving his hasty instructions to the cook, was in a soft and amiable mood, and, as Henry said to himself fifty times in the course of the morning, five pounds was five pounds. By the time ten o'clock came he could hold out no longer, and with a full sense of the favor he was about to confer, he approached the unconscious skipper.

Before he could speak he was startled by a commotion on the quay, and looking up, saw the cook, who had gone ashore for vegetables, coming full tilt towards the ship. He appeared to be laboring under strong excitement, and bumped passers-by and dropped cabbages with equal unconcern.

"What on earth's the matter with the cook," said the skipper, as the men suspended work to gaze on the approaching figure. "What's wrong?" he demanded sharply, as the cook, giving a tremendous leap on board, rushed up and spluttered in his ear.

"What?" he repeated.

The cook, with his hand on his distressed chest, gasped for breath.

"Captain Gething!" panted the cook at last, recovering his breath with an effort. "Round the— corner."

Almost as excited as the cook, the skipper sprang ashore and hurried along the quay with him, violently shaking off certain respectable citizens who sought to detain the cook, and ask him what he meant by it.

"I expect you've made a mistake," said the skipper, as they rapidly reached the small street. "Don't run—we shall have a crowd."

"If it wasn't 'im it was his twin brother," said the cook. "Ah, there he is! That's the man!"

He pointed to Henry's acquaintance of the previous day, who, with his hands in his pockets, was walking listlessly along on the other side of the road.

"You get back," said the skipper hurriedly. "You'd better run a little, then these staring idiots 'll follow you."

The cook complied, and the curious, seeing that he appeared to be the more irrational of the two, and far more likely to get into mischief, set off in pursuit. The skipper crossed the road, and began gently to overtake his quarry.

He passed him, and looking back, regarded him unobserved. The likeness was unmistakable, and for a few seconds he kept on his way in doubt how to proceed. Then he stopped, and turning round, waited till the old man should come up to him.

"Good-morning," he said pleasantly.

"Morning," said the old man, half stopping.

"I'm in a bit of a difficulty," said the skipper laughing. "I've got a message to deliver to a man in this place and I can't find him. I wonder whether you could help me."

"What's his name?" asked the other.

"Captain Gething," said the skipper.

The old man started, and his face changed to an unwholesome white. "I never heard of him," he muttered, thickly, trying to pass on.

"Nobody else seems to have heard of him either," said the skipper, turning with him; "that's the difficulty."

He waited for a reply, but none came. The old man, with set face, walked on rapidly.

"He's supposed to be in hiding," continued the skipper. "If you should ever run across him you might tell him that his wife and daughter Annis have been wanting news of him for five years, and that he's making all this trouble and fuss about a man who is as well and hearty as I am. Good-morning."

The old man stopped abruptly, and taking his outstretched hand, drew a deep breath.

"Tell him—the—man—is alive?" he said in a trembling voice.

"Just that," said the skipper gently, and seeing the working of the other's face, looked away. For a little while they both stood silent, then the skipper spoke again.

"If I take you back," he said, "I am to marry your daughter Annis." He put his hand on the old man's, and without a word the old man turned and went with him.

They walked back slowly towards the harbor, the young man talking, the old man listening. Outside the post office the skipper came to a sudden stop.

"How would it be to send a wire?" he asked.

"I think," said the old man eagerly, as he followed him in, "it would be the very thing."

He stood watching attentively as the skipper tore up form after form, meditatively sucking the chained lead pencil with a view to inspiration between whiles. Captain Gething, as an illiterate, had every sympathy with one involved in the throes of writing, and for some time watched his efforts in respectful silence. After the fifth form had rolled a little crumpled ball on to the floor, however, he interposed.

"I can't think how to put it," said the skipper apologetically. "I don't want to be too sudden, you know."

"Just so," said the other, and stood watching him until, with a smile of triumph twitching the corners of his mouth, the skipper bent down and hastily scrawled off a message.

"You've done it?" he said with relief.

"How does this strike you?" asked the skipper reading. "Your father sends love to you both."

"Beautiful," murmured Captain Gething.

"Not too sudden," said the skipper; "it doesn't say I've found you, or anything of that sort; only hints at it. I'm proud of it."

"You ought to be," said Captain Gething, who was in the mood to be pleased with anything. "Lord, how pleased they'll be, poor dears! I'm ashamed to face 'em."

"Stuff!" said the skipper, who was in high spirits, as he clapped him on the back. "What you want is a good stiff drink."

He led him into a neighboring bar, and a little later the crew of the schooner, who had been casting anxious and curious glances up the quay, saw the couple approaching them. Both captains were smoking big cigars in honor of the occasion, and Captain Gething, before going on board, halted, and in warm terms noticed the appearance of the Seamew.

The crew, pausing in their labors, looked on expectantly as they reached the deck. On the cook's face was a benevolent and proprietary smile, while Henry concealed his anguish of soul under an appearance of stoic calm.

"This is the man," said the skipper, putting his hand on the cook's shoulder, "this is the man that found you, cap'n. Smartest and best chap I ever had sail with me!"

Flushed with these praises, but feeling that he fully deserved them, the cook took the hand which Captain Gething, after a short struggle with the traditions of ship masters, extended, and shook it vigorously. Having once started, he shook hands all round, winding up with the reluctant Henry.

"Why, I've seen this boy before," he said, starting. "Had a chat with him yesterday. That's what brought me down here to-day, to see whether I couldn't find him again."

"Well I'm hanged!" said the astonished skipper. "He's as sharp as needles as a rule. What were you doing with your eyes, Henry?"

In an agony of mortification and rage, as he saw the joy depicted on the faces of the crew, the boy let the question pass. The cook, at the skipper's invitation, followed him below, his reappearance being the signal for anxious inquiries on the part of his friends. He answered them by slapping his pocket, and then thrusting his hand in produced five gold pieces. At first it was all congratulations, then Sam, after a short, hard, cough, struck a jarring note.

"Don't you wish now as you'd joined the syndikit, Dick?" he asked boldly.

"Wot?" said the cook, hastily replacing the coins.

"I arst 'im whether he was sorry 'e 'adn't joined us," said Sam, trying to speak calmly.

The cook threw out his hand and looked round appealingly to the landscape to bear witness to this appalling attempt at brigandage.

"You needn't look like that," said Sam. "Two pun ten's wot I want of you, an' I'll take it afore you lose it."

Then the cook found words, and with Dick and Henry for audience made an impassioned speech in defence of vested interests and the sacred rights of property. Never in his life had he been so fluent or so inventive, and when he wound up a noble passage on the rights of the individual, in which he alluded to Sam as a fat sharper, he felt that his case was won.

"Two pun ten," said Sam, glowering at him.

The cook, moistening his lips with his tongue, resumed his discourse.

"Two pun ten," said Sam again; "an' I don't know what you're goin' to do with your half, but I'm goin' to give ten bob to Dick."

"Why don't you give the man his money?" said Dick warmly.

"Becos the syndikit 'ad all fell through," said the cook. "The syndikit was only a syndikit when we was both looking for 'im together. If the syndikit—"

"That's enough about 'em," said Dick impatiently; "give the man 'is money. Everybody knows you was goin' shares. I'm ashamed of you, cook, I wouldn't have thought it of you."

It ended in simple division, Dick taking what was over on Sam's side and more than hinting that he was ready to do the cook a similar service. The cook turned a deaf ear, however, and declining in emphatic language to step ashore and take something, went and sulked in the galley.

At dinner-time a telegram came from Annis, and the next morning brought a letter from her which the skipper read aloud to the proud father. He read it somewhat jerkily, omitting sentences and halves of sentences which he thought might not interest the old man, or perhaps, what was more likely, would interest him a great deal. After that they were all busy taking in the cargo, Captain Gething, in shirt and trousers, insisting upon lending a hand.

The cargo was all in by five o'clock and the hatches down. Below in the cabin the two captains and the mate sat over a substantial tea.

"Get away about three, I s'pose?" said the mate.

The skipper nodded.

"Get away about three," he repeated, "and then for Northfleet. I'll have all the hands to the wedding, and you shall be best man, Jim."

"And Henry 'll be a little page in white satin knickers holding up the bride's train," said the mate, spluttering at the picture he had conjured up.

They all laughed—all except Henry, who, having come down with some hot water from the galley, surveyed the ribald scene with a scarcely concealed sneer.

Half an hour later the skipper and mate went ashore to transact a little business, leaving the old man smoking peacefully in the cabin. The crew, having adjusted their differences, had already gone ashore to treat each other to beer, leaving Henry in sole charge.

"You'll stay by the ship, boy," said the skipper, looking down on him from the quay.

"Ay, ay, sir," said Henry sulkily.

The two men walked along the quay and into the High Street, the skipper shrugging his shoulders good-naturedly as he caught, through a half-open door, a glimpse of his crew settling down to business. It was an example that in the circumstances seemed to be worth following, and at the next public-house the mate, sacrificing his inclinations to the occasion, drank port wine instead of his favorite whisky. For the same reason he put his pipe back in his pocket and accepted a cigar, and then followed his superior into the street.

"Where's a likely tailor's?" asked the skipper, looking round.

"What for?" asked the mate.

"I'm going to get some things for Cap'n Gething," said the other. "He's hardly the figure to meet his family as he is."

"Why didn't you bring him with us?" asked the mate. "How about a fit?"

"He wouldn't hear of it," said the skipper, pausing in deep contemplation of three wax boys in a tailor's window. "He's an independent sort of man; but if I buy the clothes and take 'em aboard he can hardly refuse to wear 'em."

He led the way into the shop and asked to see some serge suits. At the mate's instigation he asked to see some more. At the mate's further instigation he asked whether that was all they had got, and being told that it was, looked at them all over again. It is ever a difficult thing to fit an absent man, but he and the mate tried on every jacket in the hope of finding a golden mean, until the mate, dropping his lighted cigar in the coat-sleeve of one, and not finding it as soon as the tailor could have desired, the latter lost all patience and insisted upon their taking that one.

"It's all right," said the mate, as they left the shop with the parcel; "it's only the lining. I'd fixed my mind on that one, too, from the first."

"Well, why didn't you say so, then?" said the skipper.

"Got it cheaper," said the mate, with a wink. "I'd bet you, if it could only be known, if we'd been suited at first he'd ha' wanted ten bob more for it."

It was quite dark by now, and after buying a cap and one or two other small articles, the mate led the way into a tavern for another drink.

"There's no hurry," he said, putting his share of bundles on the table with some relief. "What's your poison this time, cap'n?"

CHAPTER XII

In less rapid times, before the invention of the electric telegraph and other scientific luxuries, Captain Gething would have remained quietly on board the Seamew, and been delivered to his expectant family without any further trouble. As it was, the message in which Captain Wilson took such pride, reached Mrs. Gething just as Mr. Glover—who had been sitting in her parlor all the afternoon, listening as patiently as he could to her somewhat uninteresting conversation—was on the point of departure. The effect on him was hardly less marked than on his hostess, and he went on his way to the railway station in a condition in which rage and jealousy strove for the mastery. All the way to town he pondered over ways and means to wrest from his rival the prize which he had won, and by the time the train had reached Fenchurch Street he had hatched as pleasant a little plot as ever occurred to a man, most of whose existence had been spent amid the blameless surroundings of ladies' hosiery. Half an hour later he was sitting in the dingy furnished apartments of a friend of his who lived in a small house off the Walworth Road.

"I want you to do me a favor, Tillotson," he said to the unkempt-looking tenant.

"I shall be delighted," said Mr. Tillotson, sticking his hands in his pockets, and warming himself comfortably at a fire-stove ornament trimmed with red paper roses—"if I can, you know."

"It is a great favor," said Glover.

Mr. Tillotson, looking very despondent, said, of course, that would please him more.

"I wouldn't ask anybody but you to do it," said the wily Glover. "If it comes off all right I will get you that berth you asked me for at Leatham and Roberts'."

"It's coming off, then," said Mr. Tillotson, brightening visibly. "If you will wait a minute—if the girl is in I will ask her if she will go and get us something to drink."

"I had better begin at the beginning," said Mr. Glover, as, all the 'ifs' having been triumphantly surmounted, he helped himself from a small flat bottle of whiskey; "it won't take long."

He lit his pipe, and, plunging into his story, finished it without interruption.

"You are a deep one, Glover," said his admiring friend when he had finished. "I thought you had been very smart lately—not but what you were always a dressy man," he added thoughtfully.

"I believe in keeping my own things to myself," said Glover.

"And this bargee has got the old un," said Tillotson, using the terms Glover had employed in his narrative. "I don't see what is to be done, Glover."

"I want to get him away," said the other. "If I can't find him, nobody else shall, and I want you to help me."

"Go down to Stourwich, tie him up in a sack, and drown him, I suppose," said Tillotson, trying to live up to a reputation several lady friends had bestowed upon him of being sarcastic.

"Can you get away to-morrow?" demanded Glover impatiently.

"I am as free as the birds of the air," responded Tillotson gloomily; "the only difference is, nobody puts out crumbs for me."

"I can reckon on you, then," said Glover. "I thought I could. We have known each other a long time, Tillotson. There is nothing like an old friend when one is in trouble."

Mr. Tillotson assented modestly. "You won't forget about Leatham and Roberts?" he said.

"Of course not," said Glover. "You see, it won't do to be seen in this thing myself. What I want you to do is to come down with me to Stourwich and bring the old man to London; then I can find him at my own time, in the street or anywhere, quite haphazard like."

"I don't quite see how it is to be done," said Tillotson.

"Meet me to-morrow morning at Waterloo, at ten minutes past eight," said Glover, finishing his glass and rising; "and we will have a try, at any rate."

He shook hands with his friend, and following him down the uncarpeted stairs, said a few words at the door in favor of early rising, and departed to his place of business to make his own arrangements about the morrow.

He was at the station and in the train first in the morning, Mr. Tillotson turning up with that extreme punctuality which enables a man to catch his train before it has got up full speed.

"I was half afraid at one time that I shouldn't have done it," said Mr. Tillotson, in self-congratulation, as he fell on to the seat. "Smoker, too! Couldn't have done better if I had been here at seven o'clock."

His friend grunted, and, there being nobody else in the carriage, began at once to discuss the practical part of the business.

"If he could only read we might send a letter aboard to him," said Mr. Tillotson, pushing his hat back. "The idea of a man his age not being able to!"

"He's one of the old school," said Glover.

"Funny sort of school," said Tillotson flippantly. "Well, we must take our chance of him going for a walk, I suppose."

They reached Stourwich soon after midday, and Glover, keeping a wary look out for Wilson, proceeded slowly to the quay with his friend, leaving the latter to walk down and discover the schooner while he went and hired a first-floor room at the "Royal Porpoise," a little bow-windowed tavern facing the harbor.

"That's the one," said Mr. Tillotson, as he joined his friend upstairs and led him to the window; "that little craft there. See that old chap working with the rest?"

Mr. Glover, who was focussing a pair of cheap field-glasses on to the schooner, gave a little exclamation of surprise.

"That's him, sure enough," he said, putting down the glasses. "Now what are we to do?"

At Tillotson's suggestion they had some dinner, and Glover fumed the afternoon away, while his friend hung about the quay. After tea his impatience got the better of his caution, and, pulling his hat over his eyes, he went on the quay too. Fifty yards beyond the Seamew he found a post, and leaning against it with his friend, anxiously watched the deck of the schooner.

"There's three of 'em going ashore," said Tillotson suddenly. "Look!"

They watched breathlessly as the crew walked slowly off, and, dusk coming on, approached a little closer.

"There's that fellow Wilson," said Glover, in a whisper. "Don't look!"

"Well, what's the use of telling me?" said Tillotson reasonably.

"He's going ashore with another chap," continued Glover excitedly— "the mate, I expect. Now's your chance. Get him away, and I'll stand you something handsome—upon my soul I will!"

"What do you call something handsome?" inquired Tillotson, whose pulse was not so feverish as his friend's.

"Get him safe to London and I'll stand a fiver," said Glover. "Now go. I'll stay here."

Mr. Tillotson, having got matters on a business footing, went, and, carelessly twisting his small moustache, slowly approached the schooner, on the deck of which was a small boy.

"Is Captain Gething aboard, old man?" inquired Mr. Tillotson, in a friendly voice.

"Down the cabin, I b'lieve," said Henry, jerking his thumb.

"I should like to see him," said Mr. Tillotson.

"I've got no objection," said Henry.

Charmed with his success, Mr. Tillotson stepped aboard and looked carelessly round.

"He's an old friend of mine," he said confidentially. "What's that you're smoking?"

"Shag," was the reply.

"Try a cigar," said Mr. Tillotson, producing three in an envelope. "You'll find them rather good."

The gratified Henry took one, and, first crackling it against his ear, smelt it knowingly, while Mr. Tillotson, in a leisurely fashion, descended to the cabin.

A tea-tray and an untidy litter of cups and saucers stood on the table, at the end of which sat an old man with his folded hands resting on the table.

"Good-evening," said Mr. Tillotson, pausing at the doorway and peering through the gloom to make sure that there was nobody else present. "All alone?"

"All alone," repeated Captain Gething, looking up and wondering who this might be.

"It's too dark to see you far," said Tillotson, in a mysterious whisper, "but it's Captain Gething, ain't it?"

"That's me," said the Captain uneasily.

"Going to Northfleet?" inquired Mr. Tillotson in another whisper.

"What do you mean?" inquired the captain quickly, as he gripped the edges of the table.

"Are you sure it'll be all right?" continued Tillotson.

"What do you mean?" repeated the captain from his seat. "Speak plain."

"I mean that you had better bolt," said Tillotson in a hurried whisper. "There's a heavy reward out for you, which Captain Wilson wants. You can't do what you did for nothing, you know."

Captain Gething sat down in his seat again and shaded his face with his hand.

"I'll go back," he said brokenly. "Wilson told me he was alive, and that it was all a mistake. If he's lying to me for the price of my old neck, let him have it."

"What about your wife and daughter?" said Tillotson, who was beginning to have a strong disrelish for his task. "I saw in the paper last night that Wilson had got you. He's gone ashore now to make arrangements at the station."

"He had a letter from my daughter this morning, said the old man brokenly.

"He told you it was from her," said Tillotson. "Get your things and come quick."

Excited by the part he was playing, he bent forward and clutched at the old man's arm. Captain Gething, obedient to the touch, rose, and taking his battered cap from a nail, followed him in silence above.

"We're going for a drink," said Tillotson to the boy. "We'll be back in ten minutes."

"All right," said Henry cheerfully; "wish I was going with you."

The other laughed airily, and gaining the quay, set off with the silent old man by his side. At first the captain went listlessly enough, but as he got farther and farther from the ship all the feelings of the hunted animal awoke within him, and he was as eager to escape as Tillotson could have wished.

"Where are we going?" he inquired as they came in sight of the railway station. "I'm not going by train."

"London," said Tillotson. "That's the most like-ly place to get lost in."

"I'm not going in the train," said the other doggedly.

"Why not?" said Tillotson in surprise.

"When they come back to the ship and find me gone they'll telegraph to London," said the old man. "I won't be caught like a rat in a trap."

"What are you going to do, then?" inquired the perplexed Tillotson.

"I don't know," said the old man. "Walk, I think. It's dark, and we might get twenty miles away before daybreak."

"Yes, we might," said Tillotson, who had no fancy for a nocturnal pilgrimage of the kind; "but we're not going to."

"Let me go alone," said the old man.

Tillotson shook his head.

"They'd be bound to spot you tramping about the country," he said confidently. "Now do let me know what's best for you, and go by train."

"I won't," said Gething obstinately. "You've been very kind, more than kind, in giving me warning. Let me go off by myself."

Tillotson shook his head and glanced carelessly in the direction of Glover, who was some few yards behind.

"I wish you'd trust me," he said earnestly. "You'll be safer in London than anywhere."

Captain Gething pondered. "There's a schooner about half a mile up the river, which is getting away about one o'clock this morning," he said slowly. "I've worked on her once or twice, and the skipper might take us if you can pay him well. He knows me as Stroud."

"If you'll wait here a minute or two I'll go to the railway station and get my bag," said Tillotson, who wanted to confer with his chief.

"I'll wait up the road under the arch," said Cap-tain Gething.

"Now don't run away," said Tillotson impressively. "If you won't go by train, perhaps the schooner is the best thing we can do."

He set off to the station, and after a hurried consultation with Glover, returned anxiously to the arch. Gething, standing in the shadow with his hands in his pockets, was patiently waiting.

"It's all right," said Tillotson cheerfully; "and now for a sea voyage. You know the way to the schooner, I suppose."

They made their way back cautiously, Captain Gething turning off to the left before they reached the harbor and leading the way through dingy little streets of private houses and chandlers' shops. It was not a part usually frequented by people taking an evening stroll, and Henry, who had begun to get uneasy at their absence, and starting in search of them had picked them up at the corner, followed wondering.

His wonder increased as they left the houses and met the cool air blowing from the river. The road was dark and uneven, and he followed cautiously, just keeping them in sight, until at a tumble-down little wharf they halted, and after a low consultation, boarded a small schooner lying alongside. There was nobody on the deck, but a light showed in the cabin, and after a minute's hesitation they went below.

An hour or two passed, and the small watcher, ensconced behind a pile of empties, shivered with the cold. Unconscious of the amicable overtures in the cabin, which had resulted in the master of the Frolic taking a couple of cabin passengers who were quite willing to rough it in the matter of food and accommodation, and willing to pay for it, he was afraid to desert his post. Another hour passed. A couple of seamen came by his place of concealment, and stepping aboard, went down the foc'sle. A clock struck eleven, and a few minutes later the light in the cabin was extinguished.

The boy watched another quarter of an hour and then, the ship being dark and still, crept noiselessly on board. The sound of deep snoring came from the cabin, and gaining the wharf again, he set off as hard as he could run to the Seamew.

CHAPTER XIII

Wilson and the mate returned to the ship laden with their spoils, and pitching them on board first, descended themselves by a slower but pleasanter method.

"I expect our chaps are all ashore still," said the mate, looking round. "Pretty state they'll be in for a start. I suppose the boy's down with the cap'n."

"Just go down and send him up," said the skipper; "it's rather a delicate thing to do to give a man a suit of clothes. I don't want anybody standing round."

"There's no light," said the mate, looking towards the skylight. He went below and felt his way into the cabin.

"All in the dark?" he said cheerfully.

There was no reply. He fumbled about in the darkness for the matches, and having obtained them, struck a light and looked round. The cabin was empty. He opened the door of the state-room and peered in; that too was empty.

"He must have gone for a walk with the boy," said the skipper uneasily when he returned with the news.

He took up the parcel again and went below, followed by the mate, and for some time sat silently smoking.

"Nine o'clock," said the mate at last in consternation as the little clock tinkled the hour. "That confounded boy's not up to any mischief, I s'pose? He's been in a devil of a temper the last day or two."

"I don't see what mischief he could do," pondered the other, knitting his brows.

"Look's to me as if he's spirited him away," continued the mate. "I'll go ashore and have a look round and see whether I can see anything of them."

He took his cap from the locker and went. An hour elapsed, and the skipper, a prey to great anxiety, went up on deck.

The shops had closed, and with the exception of the street lamps, the town was in darkness and the streets silent, except for a chance wayfarer. Two or three seamen came up the quay and went aboard the steamer in the next berth. A woman came slowly along, peering in an uncertain fashion at the various craft, and shrinking back as a seaman passed her. Abreast of the Seamew she stopped, and in the same doubtful manner looked down on the deck. The skipper crossed to the side, and straining his eyes through the gloom, looked up at her.

"Is this the Seamew?" inquired a fresh girlish voice.

"Annis!" shouted the astounded skipper. "Annis!"

He ran up the rigging, and stepping on to the quay seized her hand. Then he drew her unresistingly towards him and was in the act of passing his arm round her waist when he remembered his position and drew back awkwardly.

"Come on board," he said gently.

He straddled from the quay to the rigging, and extending his hand in the midst of a perfect silence, helped her to the deck.

"Where is my father?" she said eagerly.

Wilson made no reply.

"Where is he?" she repeated.

Wilson shook his head. "I don't know," he said gloomily, "I don't know. He was here an hour or two ago. He was here yesterday."

She caught his arm breathlessly.

"Where is he now? What have you done with him?"

Wilson told her all he knew and having finished, watched her anxiously as she drew back a little and tapped on the deck with her foot.

A badly-blended chorus, making up in strength what it lacked in harmony, sounded on the quay, and gradually coming nearer, stopped at the Seamew for a final shout. The finale was rendered by the cook and Dick with much vehemence, while Sam, excited by his potations, danced madly before them.

"Silence up there!" shouted the skipper sternly, as Annis shrank away.

"A' right, sir," hiccupped Dick solemnly. "I'm lookin' after them. Mind how you break your neck, Sam."

Thus adjured, Sam balanced himself on the edge of the quay, and executing a double shuffle on the very brink of it by way of showing his complete mastery over his feet, fell into the rigging and descended. He was followed by Dick and the cook, both drunk, and both preternaturally solemn.

"Get below," said the skipper sharply.

"Ay, ay, sir," said Dick, with a lurch. "Come on, Sam, we—ain't wanted—here."

"It's all your damned dancing, Sam!" said the cook—who had ever an eye for beauty—plaintively.

"Will you get below?" roared the maddened skipper, giving him a push.

"I'm very sorry," he said, turning to Annis as they disappeared; "everything seems to be going wrong to-night."

"It doesn't matter," she said coldly. "Goodnight."

"Where are you going?" asked Wilson.

"Going to find a hotel," said Annis; "there's no train back to-night."

"Take the cabin," he said entreatingly, "I and the mate'll sleep for'ard."

"No, thank you," said Annis.

She stepped to the side, and, assisted by the skipper, clambered up on to the quay again. The mate came up at the moment and stood eyeing her curiously.

"This is Miss Gething," said the skipper slowly. "Any news?"

"None," said the mate solemnly; "they've vanished like smoke."

"Is it certain," asked Annis, addressing, him, "that it was my father?"

The mate looked at the skipper and pushed his cap back. "We had no reason to think otherwise," he said shortly. "It's a mystery to me altogether. He can't have gone home by train because he had no money."

"It couldn't have been my father," said Annis slowly. "Somebody has been deceiving you. Good-night. I will come round in the morning; it is getting late."

"Where are you going?" inquired the mate.

"She's going to look for a hotel," said the skipper, answering for her.

"It's late," said the mate dubiously, "and this isn't much of a place for hotels. Why not take her to the woman where her father has been staying? You said she seemed a decent sort."

"It's a poor place," began the other.

"That'll do," said Annis decidedly; "if it was good enough for my father it is good enough for me. If it wasn't my father I may learn something about him. Is it far?"

"Two miles," said the mate.

"We'd better start at once, then," said the skipper, moving a step or two by way of example.

"And perhaps you'll walk down too," said Annis to the mate.

It went to the mate's heart to do it, but he was a staunch friend. "No, I think I'll turn in," he said, blushing at his rudeness; "I'm tired."

He lifted his cap awkwardly and descended. Annis, with her head at an uncomfortable altitude, set off with the skipper.

"I'm sorry the mate wouldn't come," said the latter stiffly.

After this they went on in silence along the quiet road, Miss Gething realizing instinctively that the man by her side had got a temper equal to at least a dozen of her own. This made her walk a little closer to him, and once, ever so lightly, her hand brushed against his. The skipper put his hands in his jacket pockets.

They reached the late habitation of the mysterious Captain Gething without another word having been spoken on the journey. The mews was uninviting enough by daylight, by night it was worse. The body of a defunct four-wheeler blocked up half the entrance, and a retriever came out of his kennel at the other end and barked savagely.

"That's the house," said Wilson, indicating it—"number five. What's the matter?"

For Miss Gething, after making little dabs with her handkerchief at lips which did not require the attention, was furtively applying it to eyes which did.

"I'm tired," she said softly—"tired and disappointed."

She hesitated a moment, and then before Wilson had quite made up his mind what to do, moved proudly away and knocked at the door of number five. It was opened after some delay by an untidy woman in crackers and a few other things, who having listened to the skipper's explanation, admitted Miss Gething to her father's room. She then saw the skipper to the door again, and having wished him a somewhat grim good-night, closed the door.

He walked back as sharply as he could to the schooner, his mind in a whirl with the events of the evening, and as he neared the quay broke into a run, in awkward imitation of a small figure approaching from the opposite direction.

"You little vagabond!" he panted, seizing him by the collar as they reached the schooner together.

"A'right," said Henry; "'ave it your own way then."

"Drop him overboard," said the mate, who was standing on the deck.

Henry indulged in a glance of contempt—made safe by the darkness—at this partisan, and with the air of one who knows that he has an interesting yarn to spin, began at the beginning and worked slowly up for his effects. The expediency of brevity and point was then tersely pointed out to him by both listeners, the highly feminine trait of desiring the last page first being strongly manifested.

"I can't make head or tail of it," said the skipper, after the artist had spoilt his tale to suit his public. "He's taken fright at something or other. Well, we'll go after him."

"They're getting away at about one," said the mate; "and suppose he won't come, what are you going to do then? After all, it mightn't be her father. Damned unsatisfactory I call it!"

"I don't know what to do," said the bewildered skipper; "I don't know what's best."

"Well, it ain't my business," said Henry, who had been standing by silently; "but I know what I should do."

Both men leaned forward eagerly.

"I may be a young vagabond," said Henry, enjoying to the full this tribute to his powers—"p'raps I am. I may be put to bed by a set of grinning idiots; I may—"

"What would you do, Henry?" asked the skipper very quietly.

"Go back an' fetch Miss Gething, o' course," said the boy, "an' take her down to the ship. That'll settle it."

"By Jove! the boy's right," said the mate—"if there's time."

But the skipper had already started.

"You're a very good boy, Henry," said the mate approvingly. "Now go down and watch the Frolic again, and as soon as she starts getting under way run back and let us know. If she passes before he comes back I'll hail her and try and find out what it all means."

Meantime the skipper, half walking, half running, went on his way to Overcourt, arriving at Stagg's Gardens in a breathless condition. Number five was fast asleep when he reached it and began a violent thumping upon the door.

"Who's there? What do you want?" demanded a shrill voice as the window was thrown up and a female head protruded.

"I want to see that young lady I brought here a little while ago," said the skipper—"quick."

"What, at this time o' night!" said the lady. "Be reasonable, young man, if you are sweethearting."

"Something important," said the skipper impatiently.

"Can't you tell me what it is?" said the lady, who felt that she was in a position to have her curiosity satisfied.

"Tell her I've got news of her father," said the skipper, restraining himself with difficulty.

The head disappeared and the window was closed. After what seemed an hour to the impatient man, he heard a step in the passage, the door opened, and Annis stood before him.

With a very few words they were walking together again down the road, Annis listening to his story as they went. It was a long way, and she was already tired, but she refused the offer of her companion's arm with a spirit which showed that she had not forgotten the previous journey. As they neared the Seamew the skipper's spirits sank, for the mate, who was watching, ran out to meet them.

"It's no use," he said sympathetically; "she's under way. Shall we hail her as she goes by?"

The skipper, leaving Annis unceremoniously on the quay, sprang aboard and peered anxiously down the river. The night was starlit, and he could just discern a craft coming slowly towards them.

"Hoist a couple of lanterns, Jack, and call the crew up quickly," he cried to the mate.

"What for?" said the other in astonishment.

"You light 'em," cried the skipper excitedly. "Henry, help me off with these hatches."

He was down on his knees with the boy unfastening them, while the mate, having lit a lantern, ran forward to rouse the men. The Frolic was now but twenty yards astern.

"Ahoy! schooner, ahoy!" bawled Wilson, running suddenly to the side.

"Halloa!" came a hoarse voice.

"Are you full up?" shouted the master of the Seamew.

"No," came the roar again.

"Drop your anchor and come alongside," shouted the skipper, "I've got to stay here another week, and I've got a dozen barrels o' herring must be in London before then."

The Frolic was abreast of them, and he held his breath with suspense.

"It won't take you half an hour," he shouted anxiously.

The grating of the cable was music in his ears as it ran out, and hardly able to believe in the success of his scheme he saw the crew taking in the sail they had just begun to set. Ten minutes later the Frolic was rubbing against his side.

The hatches were off the Seamew, and a lantern swinging in her hold shed a sickly light upon the sleepy faces of her crew. The mate was at the foc'sle whispering instructions to Annis.

"Look alive," said the master of the Frolic, "I'll just take 'em on deck for the present."

He came fussily to the side to superintend, gazing curiously at Annis, who was standing watching the operations.

"What a nice ship!" she said. "May I come on board?"

"You're quite welcome if you don't get in the way," was the reply.

Accepting this qualified permission, Annis stepped on board and walked quietly round the deck. At the companion she paused and looked round. Everybody was busy; and trembling with nervousness, she hesitated a moment and then descended into the dark cabin.

"That you, captain?" said a voice. "What are we stopping for?"

Annis made no reply.

"Who is it?" said the voice again.

"Hush!" said Annis.

"Oh, all right," said Mr. Tillotson shortly. "What's wrong?"

Annis hesitated, waiting to hear another voice, but in vain. She fancied that she heard another person breathing, but that was all.

"Father!" she cried, suddenly. "It's me! Annis! Where are you?"

There was a great shout from the other side of the cabin, and in the gloom she saw something spring up and come towards her. Something which caught her in a mighty grasp and crushed her soft face against a long, stiff beard. Laughing and crying together she put her arms about its neck and clung to it convulsively.

"There, there, my lass!" said Captain Gething at last.

"We only stopped you by a miracle," said Annis hysterically. "The Seamew is alongside, and why you wanted to run away again I don't know."

"I don't understand," said Captain Gething wearily.

"You can understand that I wouldn't take you into danger," said Annis tenderly. "Put your coat on and come with me."

Without another word Captain Gething did as he was bid. He stopped, as though to speak to Tillotson, and then thinking better of it, followed his daughter on deck.

"I'm not coming with you, cap'n," he said as that ardent mariner passed them rolling a barrel along the deck.

"A' right," said the other briefly; "you won't get your money back."

In a shamefaced fashion Captain Gething, still holding his daughter's arm, stepped on board the Seamew and shook hands with its master. By the time he was half through his story there was a burning desire on the part of the skipper to go down and have a look at Tillotson—a desire peremptorily checked by Annis, who had an erroneous opinion concerning that gentleman's identity, and the Frolic having taken in its herrings, sheered off with a friendly good-night. The crew of the Seamew watched her until she had her anchor up, and then, at the impatient suggestion of Henry, who was stage managing, went below.

"Are you satisfied now?" inquired Wilson in a low voice, as Captain Gething, with a wisdom born of years, went slowly below.

"Quite," breathed Annis softly.

"I'm not," said Wilson, in tones full of meaning.

Miss Gething smiled, and leaning against the side surveyed, with some interest, the dark water and the sleeping town. She did not move when Wilson came and stood by her, and when he took her hand, made no protest.

"I'm not satisfied—yet," said Wilson, raising her hand to his lips.

His eye caught the two lanterns which were burning somewhat garishly, and crossing over, he took them down and blew them out. He turned suddenly at the sound of a smothered laugh, a moment too late. Annis Gething had gone below.

THE BROWN MAN'S SERVANT

CHAPTER I

The shop of Solomon Hyams stood in a small thoroughfare branching off the Commercial Road. In its windows unredeemed pledges of all kinds, from old-time watches to seamen's boots, appealed to all tastes and requirements. Bundles of cigars, candidly described as "wonderful," were marked at absurdly low figures, while silver watches endeavored to excuse the clumsiness of their make by describing themselves as "strong workmen's." The side entrance, up a narrow alley, was surmounted by the usual three brass balls, and here Mr. Hyams' clients were wont to call. They entered as optimists, smiled confidently upon Mr. Hyams, argued, protested shrilly, and left the establishment pessimists of a most pronounced and virulent type.

None of these things, however, disturbed the pawnbroker. The drunken client who endeavored to bail out his Sunday clothes with a tram ticket was accommodated with a chair, while the assistant went to hunt up his friends and contract for a speedy removal; the old woman who, with a view of obtaining a higher advance than usual, poured a tale of grievous woe into the hardened ears of Mr. Hyams, found herself left to the same invaluable assistant, and, realizing her failure, would at once become cheerful and take what was offered. Mr. Hyams' methods of business were quiet and unostentatious, and rumor had it that he might retire at any time and live in luxury.

It was a cold, cheerless afternoon in November as Mr. Hyams, who had occasional hazy ideas of hygiene, stood at his door taking the air. It was an atmosphere laden with soot and redolent of many blended odors, but after the fusty smell of the shop it was almost health-giving. In the large public-house opposite, with its dirty windows and faded signboards, the gas was already being lit, which should change it from its daylight dreariness to a resort of light and life.

Mr. Hyams, who was never in a hurry to light up his own premises, many of his clients preferring the romantic light which comes between day and night for their visits, was about to leave the chilly air for the warmth inside, when his attention was attracted by a seaman of sturdy aspect stopping and looking in at his window. Mr. Hyams rubbed his hands softly. There was an air of comfort and prosperity about this seaman, and the pawnbroker had many small articles in his window, utterly useless to the man, which he would have liked to have sold him.

The man came from the window, made as though to pass, and then paused irresolute before the pawn-broker.

"You want a watch?" said the latter genially. "Come inside."

Mr. Hyams went behind his counter and waited.

"I don't want to buy nothing, and I don't want to pawn nothing," said the sailor. "What do you think o' that?"

Mr. Hyams, who objected to riddles, especially those which seemed to be against business, eyed him unfavorably from beneath his shaggy eyebrows.

"We might have a little quiet talk together," said the seaman, "you an' me; we might do a little bit o' business together, you an' me. In the parler, shall we say, over a glass o' something hot?"

Mr. Hyams hesitated. He was not averse to a little business of an illicit nature, but there rose up vividly before him the picture of another sailor who had made much the same sort of proposal, and, after four glasses of rum, had merely suggested to him that he should lend him twenty pounds on the security of an I.O.U. It was long since, but the memory of it still rankled.

"What sort of business is it?" he inquired.

"Business that's too big for you, p'raps," said the sailor with a lordly air. "I'll try a bigger place. What's that lantern-faced swab shoving his ugly mug into the daylight for?"

"Get off," said the pawnbroker to the assistant, who was quietly and unobtrusively making a third.

"Mind the shop. This gentleman and I have business in the parlor. Come this way, sir."

He raised the flap of the counter, and led the way to a small, untidy room at the back of the shop. A copper kettle was boiling on the fire, and the table was already laid for tea. The pawnbroker, motioning his visitor to a dingy leather armchair, went to a cupboard and produced a bottle of rum, three parts full, and a couple of glasses.

"Tea for me," said the seaman, eyeing the bottle wistfully.

The pawnbroker pricked up his ears. "Nonsense," he said, with an attempt at heartiness, "a jolly fellow like you don't want tea. Have some o' this."

"Tea, confound yer!" said the other. "When I say tea, I mean tea."

The pawnbroker, repressing his choler, replaced the bottle, and, seating himself at the table, reached over for the kettle, and made the tea. It was really a pleasing picture of domestic life, and would have looked well in a lantern slide at a temperance lecture, the long, gaunt Jew and the burly seaman hobnobbing over the blameless teapot. But Mr. Hyams grew restless. He was intent upon business; but the other, so far as his inroads on the teapot and the eatables gave any indication, seemed to be bent only upon pleasure. Once again the picture of the former sailor rose before Mr. Hyams' eyes, and he scowled fiercely as the seaman pushed his cup up for the fourth time.

"And now for a smoke," said his visitor, as he settled back in his chair. "A good 'un, mind. Lord, this is comfort! It's the first bit o' comfort I've 'ad since I come ashore five days ago."

The pawnbroker grunted, and producing a couple of black, greasy-looking cigars, gave one to his guest. They both fell to smoking, the former ill at ease, the latter with his feet spread out on the small fender, making the very utmost of his bit of comfort.

"Are you a man as is fond of asking questions?" he said at length.

"No," said the pawnbroker, shutting his lips illustratively.

"Suppose," said the sailor, leaning forward intently—"suppose a man came to you an' ses— there's that confounded assistant of yours peeping through the door."

The pawnbroker got up almost as exasperated as the seaman, and, after rating his assistant through the half-open door, closed it with a bang, and pulled down a small blind over the glass.

"Suppose a man came to you," resumed the sailor, after the pawnbroker had seated himself again, "and asked you for five hundred pounds for something. Have you got it?"

"Not here," said the pawnbroker suspiciously. "I don't keep any money on the premises."

"You could get it, though?" suggested the other.

"We'll see," said the pawnbroker; "five hundred pounds is a fortune—five hundred pounds, why it takes years of work—five hundred pounds—"

"I don't want no blessed psalms," said the seaman abruptly; "but, look here, suppose I wanted five hundred pounds for something, and you wouldn't give it. How am I to know you wouldn't give information to the police if I didn't take what you offered me for it?"

The pawnbroker threw up his huge palms in virtuous horror.

"I'd mark you for it if you did," said the seaman menacingly, through his teeth. "It 'ud be the worst day's work you ever did. Will you take it or leave it at my price, an' if you won't give it, leave me to go as I came?"

"I will," said the pawnbroker solemnly.

The seaman laid his cigar in the tray, where it expired in a little puddle of tea, and, undoing his coat, cautiously took from his waist a canvas belt In a hesitating fashion he dangled the belt in his hands, looking from the Jew to the door, and from the door back to the Jew again. Then from a pocket in the belt he took something wrapped in a small piece of dirty flannel, and, unrolling it, deposited on the table a huge diamond, whose smouldering fires flashed back in many colors the light from the gas.

The Jew, with an exclamation, reached forward to handle it, but the sailor thrust him back.

"Hands off," he said grimly. "None of your ringing the changes on me."

He tipped it over with his finger-nail on the table from side to side, the other, with his head bent down, closely inspecting it. Then, as a great indulgence, he laid it on the Jew's open palm for a few seconds.

"Five hundred pounds," he said, taking it in his own hands again.

The pawnbroker laughed. It was a laugh which he kept for business purposes, and would have formed a valuable addition to the goodwill of the shop.

"I'll give you fifty," he said, after he had regained his composure.

The seaman replaced the gem in its wrapper again.

"Well, I'll give you seventy, and risk whether I lose over it," continued the pawnbroker.

"Five hundred's my price," said the seaman calmly, as he placed the belt about his waist and began to buckle it up.

"Seventy-five," said the pawnbroker persuasively.

"Look here," said the seaman, regarding him sternly, "you drop it. I'm not going to haggle with you. I'm not going to haggle with any man. I ain't no judge o' diamonds, but I've 'ad cause to know as this is something special. See here."

He rolled back the coat sleeve from his brawny arm, and revealed a long, newly healed scar.

"I risked my life for that stone," he said slowly. "I value my life at five hundred pounds. It's likely worth more than as many thousands, and you know it. However, good-night to you, mate. How much for the tea?"

He put his hand contemptuously in his trouser pocket, and pulled out some small change.

"There's the risk of getting rid of the stone," said the pawnbroker, pushing aside the proffered coin. "Where did it come from? Has it got a history?"

"Not in Europe it ain't," said the seaman. "So far as I know, you an' me an' one other are the only white men as know of it. That's all I'm going to tell you."

"Do you mind waiting while I go and fetch a friend of mine to see it?" inquired the pawnbroker. "You needn't be afraid," he added hastily. "He's a respectable man and as close as the grave."

"I'm not afraid," said the seaman quietly. "But no larks, mind. I'm not a nice man to play them on. I'm pretty strong, an' I've got something else besides."

He settled himself in the armchair again, and accepting another cigar, watched his host as he took his hat from the sideboard.

"I'll be back as soon as I can," said the latter somewhat anxiously. "You won't go before I come?"

"Not me," said the seaman bluntly. "When I say a thing I stick to it. I don't haggle, and haggle, and—" he paused a moment for a word, "and haggle," he concluded.

Left to himself, he smoked on contentedly, blandly undisturbed by the fact that the assistant looked in at the door occasionally, to see that things were all right. It was quite a new departure for Mr.

Hyams to leave his parlor to a stranger, and the assistant felt a sense of responsibility so great that it was a positive relief to him when his master returned, accompanied by another man.

"This is my friend," said Mr. Hyams, as they entered the parlor and closed the door. "You might let him see the stone."

The seaman took off his belt again, and placing the diamond in his hand held it before the stranger who, making no attempt to take it, turned it over with his finger and examined it critically.

"Are you going to sea again just yet?" he inquired softly.

"Thursday night," said the seaman, "Five hundred is my price; p'raps he told you. I'm not going to haggle."

"Just so, just so," said the other quietly. "It's worth five hundred."

"Spoke like a man," said the seaman warmly.

"I like to deal with a man who knows his own mind," said the stranger, "it saves trouble. But if we buy it for that amount you must do one thing for us. Keep quiet and don't touch a drop of liquor until you sail, and not a word to anybody."

"You needn't be afraid o' the licker," said the sailor grimly. "I shan't touch that for my own sake."

"He's a teetotaler," explained the pawnbroker.

"He's not," said the seaman indignantly.

"Why won't you drink, then?" asked the other man.

"Fancy," said the seaman dryly, and closed his mouth.

Without another word the stranger turned to the pawnbroker, who, taking a pocket-book from his coat, counted out the amount in notes. These, after the sailor had examined them in every possible manner, he rolled up and put in his pocket, then without a word he took out the diamond again and laid it silently on the table. Mr. Hyams, his fingers trembling with eagerness, took it up and examined it delightedly.

"You've got it a bargain," said the seaman. "Good-night, gentlemen. I hope, for your sakes, nobody'll know I've parted with it. Keep your eyes open, and trust nobody. When you see black, smell mischief. I'm glad to get rid of it."

He threw his head back, and, expanding his chest as though he already breathed more freely, nodded to both men, and, walking through the shop, passed out into the street and disappeared.

Long after he had gone, the pawnbroker and his friend, Levi, sat with the door locked and the diamond before them, eagerly inspecting it.

"It's a great risk," said the pawnbroker. "A stone like that generally makes some noise."

"Anything good is risky," said the other somewhat contemptuously. "You don't expect to get a windfall like that without any drawback, do you?"

He took the stone in his hand again, and eyed it lovingly. "It's from the East somewhere," he said quietly. "It's badly cut, but it's a diamond of diamonds, a king of gems."

"I don't want any trouble with the police," said the pawnbroker, as he took it from him.

"You are talking now as though you have just made a small advance on a stolen overcoat," said his friend impatiently. "A risk like that—and you have done it before now—is a foolish one to run; the game is not worth the candle. But this—why it warms one's blood to look at it."

"Well, I'll leave it with you," said the pawnbroker. "If you do well with it I ought not to want to work any more."

The other placed it in an inside pocket, while the owner watched him anxiously.

"Don't let any accident happen to you to-night, Levi," he said nervously.

"Thanks for your concern," said Levi grimacing. "I shall probably be careful for my own sake."

He buttoned up his coat, and, drinking a glass of hot whisky, went out whistling. He had just reached the door when the pawnbroker called him back.

"If you like to take a cab, Levi," he said, in a low voice so that the assistant should not hear, "I'll pay for it."

"I'll take an omnibus," said Levi, smiling quietly. "You're getting extravagant, Hyams. Besides, fancy the humor of sitting next to a pickpocket with this on me."

He waved a cheery farewell, and the pawnbroker, watching him from the door, scowled angrily as he saw his light-hearted friend hail an omnibus at the corner and board it. Then he went back to the shop, and his everyday business of making advances on flat-irons and other realizable assets of the neighborhood.

At ten o'clock he closed for the night, the assistant hurriedly pulling down the shutters that his time for recreation might not be unduly curtailed. He slept off the premises, and the pawnbroker, after his departure, made a slight supper, and sat revolving the affairs of the day over another of his black cigars until nearly midnight. Then, well contented with himself, he went up the bare, dirty stairs to his room and went to bed, and, despite the excitement of the evening, was soon in a loud slumber, from which he was aroused by a distant and sustained knocking.

CHAPTER II

At first the noise mingled with his dreams, and helped to form them. He was down a mine, and grimy workers with strong picks were knocking diamonds from the walls, diamonds so large that he became despondent at the comparative smallness of his own. Then he awoke suddenly and sat up with a start, rubbing his eyes. The din was infernal to a man who liked to do a quiet business in an unobtrusive way. It was a knocking which he usually associated with the police, and it came from his side door. With a sense of evil strong upon him, the Jew sprang from his bed, and, slipping the catch, noiselessly opened the window and thrust his head out. In the light of a lamp which projected from the brick wall at the other end of the alley he saw a figure below.

"Hulloa!" said the Jew harshly.

His voice was drowned in the noise.

"What do you want?" he yelled. "Hulloa, there! What do you want, I say?"

The knocking ceased, and the figure, stepping back a little, looked up at the window.

"Come down and open the door," said a voice which the pawnbroker recognized as the sailor's.

"Go away," he said, in a low, stern voice. "Do you want to rouse the neighborhood?"

"Come down and let me in," said the other. "It's for your own good. You're a dead man if you don't."

Impressed by his manner the Jew, after bidding him shortly not to make any more noise, lit his candle, and, dressing hurriedly, took the light in his hand and went grumbling downstairs into the shop.

"Now, what do you want?" he said through the door.

"Let me in and I'll tell you," said the other, "or I'll bawl it through the keyhole, if you like."

The Jew, placing the candle on the counter, drew back the heavy bolts and cautiously opened the door. The seaman stepped in, and, as the other closed the door, vaulted on to the counter and sat there with his legs dangling.

"That's right," he said, nodding approvingly in the direction of the Jew's right hand. "I hope you know how to use it."

"What do you want?" demanded the other irritably, putting his hand behind him. "What time o' night do you call this for turning respectable men out of their beds?"

"I didn't come for the pleasure o' seeing your pretty face again, you can bet," said the seaman carelessly. "It's good nature what's brought me here. What have you done with that diamond?"

"That's my business," said the other. "What do you want?"

"I told you I sailed in five days," said the seaman. "Well, I got another ship this evening instead, and I sail at 6 a.m. Things are getting just a bit too thick for me, an' I thought out o' pure good nature I'd step round and put you on your guard."

"Why didn't you do so at first?" said the Jew, eyeing him suspiciously.

"Well, I didn't want to spoil a bargain," said the seaman carelessly. "Maybe, you wouldn't have bought the stone if I had told you. Mind that thing don't go off; I don't want to rob you. Point it the other way."

"There was four of us in that deal," he continued, after the other had complied with his request. "Me an' Jack Ball and Nosey Wheeler and a Burmese chap; the last I see o' Jack Ball he was quiet and peaceful, with a knife sticking in his chest. If I hadn't been a very careful man I'd have had one sticking in mine. If you ain't a very careful man, and do what I tell you, you'll have one sticking in yours."

"Speak a little more plainly," said the Jew. "Come into the parlor, I don't want the police to see a light in the shop."

"We stole it," said the seaman, as he followed the other into the little back parlor, "the four of us, from—"

"I don't want to know anything about that," interrupted the other hastily.

The sailor grinned approvingly, and continued: "Then me an' Jack being stronger than them, we took it from them two, but they got level with poor Jack. I shipped before the mast on a barque, and they came over by steamer an' waited for me."

"Well, you're not afraid of them?" said the Jew interrogatively. "Besides, a word to the police—"

"Telling 'em all about the diamond," said the seaman. "Oh, yes. Well, you can do that now if you feel so inclined. They know all about that, bless you, and, if they were had, they'd blab about the diamond."

"Have they been dogging you?" inquired the pawnbroker.

"Dogging me!" said the seaman. "Dogging's no word for it. Wherever I've been they've been my shadders. They want to hurt me, but they're careful about being hurt themselves. That's where I have the pull of them. They want the stone back first, and revenge afterwards, so I thought I'd put you on your guard, for they pretty well guess who's got the thing now. You'll know Wheeler by his nose, which is broken."

"I'm not afraid of them," said the Jew, "but thank you for telling me. Did they follow you here?"

"They're outside, I've no doubt," said the other; "but they come along like human cats—leastways, the Burmah chap does. You want eyes in the back of your head for them almost. The Burmese is an old man and soft as velvet, and Jack Ball just afore he died was going to tell me something about him. I don't know what it was; but, pore Jack, he was a superstitious sort o' chap, and I know it was something horrible. He was as brave as a lion, was Jack, but he was afraid o' that little shrivelled-up Burmese. They'll follow me to the ship to-night. If they'll only come close enough, and there's nobody nigh, I'll do Jack a good turn."

"Stay here till the morning," said the Jew.

The seaman shook his head. "I don't want to miss my ship," said he; "but remember what I've told you, and mind, they're villains, both of them, and if you are not very careful, they'll have you, sooner or later. Good-night!"

He buttoned up his coat, and leading the way to the door, followed by the Jew with the candle, opened it noiselessly, and peered carefully out right and left. The alley was empty.

"Take this," said the Jew, proffering his pistol.

"I've got one," said the seaman. "Good-night!"

He strode boldly up the alley, his footsteps sounding loudly in the silence of the night. The Jew watched him to the corner, and then, closing the door, secured it with extra care, and went back to his bedroom, where he lay meditating upon the warning which had just been given to him until he fell asleep.

Before going downstairs next morning he placed the revolver in his pocket, not necessarily for use, but as a demonstration of the lengths to which he was prepared to go. His manner with two or three inoffensive gentlemen of color was also somewhat strained. Especially was this the case with a worthy Lascar, who, knowing no English, gesticulated cheer-fully in front of him with a long dagger which he wanted to pawn.

The morning passed without anything happening, and it was nearly dinner-time before anything occurred to justify the sailor's warning. Then, happening to glance at the window, he saw between the articles which were hanging there a villainous face, the principal feature of which being strangely bent at once recalled the warning of the sailor. As he looked the face disappeared, and a moment later its owner, after furtively looking in at the side door, entered quietly.

"Morning, boss," said he.

The pawnbroker nodded and waited.

"I want to have a little talk with you, boss," said the man, after waiting for him to speak.

"All right, go on," said the other.

"What about 'im?" said the man, indicating the assistant with a nod.

"Well, what about him?" inquired the Jew.

"What I've got to say is private," said the man.

The Jew raised his eyebrows.

"You can go in and get your dinner, Bob," he said. "Now, what do you want?" he continued. "Hurry up, because I'm busy."

"I come from a pal o' mine," said the man, speaking in a low voice, "him what was 'ere last night. He couldn't come himself, so he sent me. He wants it back."

"Wants what back?" asked the Jew.

"The diamond," said the other.

"Diamond? What on earth are you talking about?" demanded the pawnbroker.

"You needn't try to come it on me," said the other fiercely. "We want that diamond back, and, mind you, we'll have it."

"You clear out," said the Jew. "I don't allow people to come threatening me. Out you go."

"We'll do more than threaten you," said the man, the veins in his forehead swelling with rage. "You've got that diamond. You got it for five 'undred pound. We'll give you that back for it, and you may think yourself lucky to get it."

"You've been drinking," said the Jew, "or somebody's been fooling you."

"Look here," said the man with a snarl, "drop it. I'm dealing fair an' square by you. I don't want to hurt a hair of your head. I'm a peaceable man, but I want my own, and, what's more, I can get it. I got the shell, and I can get the kernel. Do you know what I mean by that?"

"I don't know, and I don't care," said the Jew. He moved off a little way, and, taking some tarnished spoons from a box, began to rub them with a piece of leather.

"I daresay you can take a hint as well as anybody else," said the other. "Have you seen that before?"

He threw something on the counter, and the Jew started, despite himself, as he glanced up. It was the sailor's belt.

"That's a hint," said the man with a leer, "and a very fair one."

The Jew looked at him steadily, and saw that he was white and nervous; his whole aspect that of a man who was running a great risk for a great stake.

"I suppose," he said at length, speaking very slowly, "that you want me to understand that you have murdered the owner of this."

"Understand what you like," said the other with sullen ferocity. "Will you let us have that back again?"

"No," said the Jew explosively. "I have no fear of a dog like you; if it was worth the trouble I'd send for the police and hand you over to them."

"Call them," said the other; "do; I'll wait. But mark my words, if you don't give us the stone back you're a dead man. I've got a pal what half that diamond belongs to. He's from the East, and a bad man to cross. He has only got to wish it, and you're a dead man without his raising a finger at you. I've come here to do you a good turn; if he comes here it's all up with you."

"Well, you go back to him," jeered the Jew; "a clever man like that can get the diamond without going near it seemingly. You're wasting your time here, and it's a pity; you must have got a lot of friends."

"Well, I've warned you," said the other, "you'll have one more warning. If you won't be wise you must keep the diamond, but it won't be much good to you. It's a good stone, but, speaking for myself I'd sooner be alive without it than dead with it."

He gave the Jew a menacing glance and departed, and the assistant having by this time finished his dinner, the pawnbroker went to his own with an appetite by no means improved by his late interview.

The cat, with its fore-paws tucked beneath it, was dozing on the counter. Business had been slack that morning, and it had only been pushed off three times. It had staked out a claim on that counter some five years before, and if anything was required to convince it of the value of the possession it was the fact that it was being constantly pushed off. To a firm-minded cat this alone gave the counter a value difficult to overestimate, and sometimes an obsequious customer fell into raptures over its beauty. This was soothing, and the animal allowed customers of this type to scratch it gently behind the ear.

The cat was for the time the only occupant of the shop. The assistant was out, and the pawnbroker sat in the small room beyond, with the door half open, reading a newspaper. He had read the financial columns, glanced at the foreign intelligence, and was just about to turn to the leader when his eye was caught by the headline, "Murder in White-chapel."

He folded the paper back, and, with a chilly feeling creeping over him, perused the account. In the usual thrilling style it recorded the finding of the body of a man, evidently a sailor, behind a hoarding placed in front of some shops in course of erection. There was no clue to the victim, who had evidently been stabbed from behind in the street, and then dragged or carried to the place in which the body had been discovered.

The pockets had been emptied, and the police who regarded the crime as an ordinary one of murder and robbery, entertained the usual hopes of shortly arresting the assassins.

The pawnbroker put the paper down, and drummed on the table with his fingers. The description of the body left no room for doubt that the victim of the tragedy and the man who had sold him the diamond were identical. He began to realize the responsibilities of the bargain, and the daring of his visitor of the day before, in venturing before him almost red-handed, gave him an unpleasant idea of the lengths to which he was prepared to go. In a pleasanter direction it gave him another idea; it was strong confirmation of Levi's valuation of the stone.

"I shall see my friend again," said the Jew to himself, as he looked up from the paper. "Let him make an attempt on me and we'll see."

He threw the paper down, and, settling back in his chair, fell into a pleasing reverie. He saw his release from sordid toil close at hand. He would travel and enjoy his life. Pity the diamond hadn't come twenty years before. As for the sailor, well, poor fellow, why didn't he stay when he was asked?

The cat, still dozing, became aware of a strong strange odor. In a lazy fashion it opened one eye, and discovered that an old, shrivelled up little man, with a brown face, was standing by the counter. It watched him lazily, but warily, out of a half-closed eye, and then, finding that he appeared to be quite harmless, closed it again.

The intruder was not an impatient type of customer. He stood for some time gazing round him; then a thought struck him, and he approached the cat and stroked it with a masterly hand. Never, in the course of its life, had the animal met such a born stroker. Every touch was a caress, and a gentle thrum, thrum rose from its interior in response.

Something went wrong with the stroker. He hurt. The cat started up suddenly and jumped behind the counter. The dark gentleman smiled an evil smile, and, after waiting a little longer, tapped on the counter.

The pawnbroker came from the little room beyond, with the newspaper in his hand, and his brow darkened as he saw the customer. He was of a harsh and dominant nature, and he foresaw more distasteful threats.

"Well, what do you want?" he demanded abruptly.

"Morning, sir," said the brown man in perfect English; "fine day."

"The day's well enough," said the Jew.

"I want a little talk with you," said the other suavely, "a little, quiet, reasonable talk."

"You'd better make it short," said the Jew. "My time is valuable."

The brown man smiled, and raised his hand with a deprecatory gesture. "Many things are valuable," said he, "but time is the most valuable of all. And time to us means life."

The Jew saw the covert threat, and grew more irritable still.

"Get to your business," he said sharply.

The brown man leant on the counter, and regarded him with a pair of fierce, brown eyes, which age had not dimmed.

"You are a reasonable man," he said slowly, "a good merchant. I can see it. But sometimes a good merchant makes a bad bargain. In that case what does the good merchant do?"

"Get out of here," said the Jew angrily.

"He makes the best of it," continued the other calmly, "and he is a lucky man if he is not too late to repair the mischief. You are not too late."

The Jew laughed boisterously.

"There was a sailor once made a bad bargain," said the brown man, still in the same even tones, "and he died—of grief."

He grinned at this pleasantry until his face looked like a cracked mask.

"I read in this paper of a sailor being killed," said the Jew, holding it up. "Have you ever heard of the police, of prison, and of the hangman?"

"All of them," said the other softly.

"I might be able to put the hangman on the track of the sailor's murderer," continued the Jew grimly.

The brown man smiled and shook his head. "You are too good a merchant," he said; "besides, it would be very difficult."

"It would be a pleasure to me," said the Jew.

"Let us talk business like men, not nonsense like children," said the brown man suddenly. "You talk of hangmen. I talk of death. Well, listen. Two nights ago you bought a diamond from a sailor for five hundred pounds. Unless you give me that diamond back for the same money I will kill you."

"What?" snarled the Jew, drawing his gaunt figure to its full height. "You, you miserable mummy?"

"I will kill you," repeated the brown man calmly. "I will send death to you—death in a horrible shape. I will send a devil, a little artful, teasing devil, to worry you and kill you. In the darkness he will come and spring out on you. You had better give back the diamond, and live. If you give it back I promise you your life."

He paused, and the Jew noticed that his face had changed, and in place of the sardonic good-humor which had before possessed it, was now distorted by a devilish malice. His eyes gleamed coldly, and he snapped them quickly as he spoke.

"Well, what do you say?" he demanded.

"This," said the Jew.

He leant over the counter, and, taking the brown man's skinny throat in his great hand, flung him reeling back to the partition, which shook with his weight. Then he burst into a laugh as the being who had just been threatening him with a terrible and mysterious death changed into a little weak old man, coughing and spitting as he clutched at his throat and fought for breath.

"What about your servant, the devil?" asked the Jew maliciously.

"He serves when I am absent," said the brown man faintly. "Even now I give you one more chance. I will let you see the young fellow in your shop die first. But no, he has not offended. I will kill—"

He paused, and his eye fell on the cat, which at that moment sprang up and took its old place on the counter. "I will kill your cat," said the brown man. "I will send the devil to worry it. Watch the cat, and as its death is so shall yours be—unless—"

"Unless?" said the Jew, regarding him mockingly.

"Unless to-night before ten o'clock you mark on your door-post two crosses in chalk," said the other. "Do that and live. Watch your cat."

He pointed his lean, brown finger at the animal, and, still feeling at his throat, stepped softly to the door and passed out.

With the entrance of other customers, the pawnbroker forgot the annoyance to which he had been subjected, and attended to their wants in a spirit made liberal by the near prospect of fortune. It was certain that the stone must be of great value. With that and the money he had made by his business, he would give up work and settle down to a life of pleasant ease. So liberal was he that an elderly

Irishwoman forgot their slight differences in creeds and blessed him fervently with all the saints in the calendar.

His assistant being back in his place in the shop, the pawnbroker returned to the little sitting-room, and once more carefully looked through the account of the sailor's murder. Then he sat still trying to work out a problem; to hand the murderers over to the police without his connection with the stolen diamond being made public, and after considerable deliberation, convinced himself that the feat was impossible. He was interrupted by a slight scuffling noise in the shop, and the cat came bolting into the room, and, after running round the table, went out at the door and fled upstairs. The assistant came into the room.

"What are you worrying the thing for?" demanded his master.

"I'm not worrying it," said the assistant in an aggrieved voice. "It's been moving about up and down the shop, and then it suddenly started like that. It's got a fit, I suppose."

He went back to the shop, and the Jew sat in his chair half ashamed of his nervous credulity, listening to the animal, which was rushing about in the rooms upstairs.

"Go and see what's the matter with the thing, Bob," he cried.

The assistant obeyed, returning hastily in a minute or two, and closing the door behind him.

"Well, what's the matter?" demanded his master.

"The brute's gone mad," said the assistant, whose face was white. "It's flying about upstairs like a wild thing. Mind it don't get in, it's as bad as a mad dog."

"Oh, rubbish," said the Jew. "Cats are often like that."

"Well, I've never seen one like it before," said the other, "and, what's more, I'm not going to see that again."

The animal came downstairs, scuffling along the passage, hit the door with its head, and then dashed upstairs again.

"It must have been poisoned, or else it's mad," said the assistant. "What's it been eating, I wonder?"

The pawnbroker made no reply. The suggestion of poisoning was a welcome one. It was preferable to the sinister hintings of the brown man. But even if it had been poisoned it was a very singular coincidence, unless indeed the Burmese had himself poisoned it He tried to think whether it could have been possible for his visitor to have administered poison undetected.

"It's quiet now," said the assistant, and he opened the door a little way.

"It's all right," said the pawnbroker, half ashamed of his fears, "get back to the shop."

The assistant complied, and the Jew, after sitting down a little while to persuade himself that he really had no particular interest in the matter, rose and went slowly upstairs. The staircase was badly lighted, and half way up he stumbled on something soft.

He gave a hasty exclamation and, stooping down, saw that he had trodden on the dead cat.

CHAPTER IV

At ten o'clock that night the pawnbroker sat with his friend Levi discussing a bottle of champagne, which the open-eyed assistant had procured from the public-house opposite.

"You're a lucky man, Hyams," said his friend, as he raised his glass to his lips. "Thirty thousand pounds! It's a fortune, a small fortune," he added correctively.

"I shall give this place up," said the pawnbroker, "and go away for a time. I'm not safe here."

"Safe?" queried Levi, raising his eyebrows.

The pawnbroker related his adventures with his visitors.

"I can't understand that cat business," said Levi when he had finished. "It's quite farcical; he must have poisoned it."

"He wasn't near it," said the pawnbroker, "it was at the other end of the counter."

"Oh, hang it," said Levi, the more irritably because he could not think of any solution to the mystery. "You don't believe in occult powers and all that sort of thing. This is the neighborhood of the Commercial Road; time, nineteenth century. The thing's got on your nerves. Keep your eyes open, and stay indoors; they can't hurt you here. Why not tell the police?"

"I don't want any questions," said the pawnbroker.

"I mean, just tell them that one or two suspicious characters have been hanging round lately," said the other. "If this precious couple see that they are watched they'll probably bolt. There's nothing like a uniform to scare that sort."

"I won't have anything to do with the police," said the pawnbroker firmly.

"Well, let Bob sleep on the premises," suggested his friend.

"I think I will to-morrow," said the other. "I'll have a bed fixed up for him."

"Why not to-night?" asked Levi.

"He's gone," said the pawnbroker briefly. "Didn't you hear him shut up?"

"He was in the shop five minutes ago," said Levi.

"He left at ten," said the pawnbroker.

"I'll swear I heard somebody only a minute or two back," said Levi, staring.

"Nerves, as you remarked a little while ago," said his friend, with a grin.

"Well, I thought I heard him," said Levi. "You might just secure the door anyway."

The pawnbroker went to the door and made it fast, giving a careless glance round the dimly lighted shop as he did so.

"Perhaps you could stay to-night yourself," he said, as he returned to the sitting-room.

"I can't possibly, to-night," said the other. "By the way, you might lend me a pistol of some kind. With all these cut-throats hanging round, visiting you is a somewhat perilous pleasure. They might take it into their heads to kill me to see whether I have got the stone."

"Take your pick," said the pawnbroker, going to the shop and returning with two or three secondhand revolvers and some cartridges.

"I never fired one in my life," said Levi dubiously, "but I believe the chief thing is to make a bang. Which'll make the loudest?"

On his friend's recommendation he selected a revolver of the service pattern, and, after one or two suggestions from the pawnbroker, expressed himself as qualified to shoot anything between a chimney-pot and a paving-stone.

"Make your room-door fast to-night, and tomorrow let Bob have a bed there," he said earnestly, as he rose to go. "By the way, why not make those chalk marks on the door just for the night? You can laugh at them to-morrow. Sort of suggestion of the Passover about it, isn't there?"

"I'm not going to mark my door for all the assassins that ever breathed," said the Jew fiercely, as he rose to see the other out.

"Well, I think you're safe enough in the house," said Levi. "Beastly dreary the shop looks. To a man of imagination like myself it's quite easy to fancy that there is one of your brown friend's pet devils crouching under the counter ready to spring."

The pawnbroker grunted and opened the door.

"Poof, fog," said Levi, as a cloud streamed in. "Bad night for pistol practice. I shan't be able to hit anything."

The two men stood in the doorway for a minute, trying to peer through the fog. A heavy, measured tread sounded in the alley; a huge figure loomed up, and, to the relief of Levi, a constable halted before them.

"Thick night, sir," said he to the pawnbroker.

"Very," was the reply. "Just keep your eye on my place to-night, constable. There have been one or two suspicious-looking characters hanging about here lately."

"I will, sir," said the constable, and moved off in company with Levi.

The pawnbroker closed the door hastily behind them and bolted it securely. His friend's jest about the devil under the counter occurred to him as he eyed it, and for the first time in his life, the lonely silence of the shop became oppressive. He half thought of opening the door again and calling them back, but by this time they were out of earshot, and he had a very strong idea that there might be somebody lurking in the fog outside.

"Bah!" said he aloud, "thirty thousand pounds."

He turned the gas-jet on full—a man that had just made that sum could afford to burn a little gas—and, first satisfying himself by looking under the counter and round the shop, re-entered the sitting room.

Despite his efforts, he could not get rid of the sense of loneliness and danger which possessed him. The clock had stopped, and the only sound audible was the snapping of the extinguished coals in the grate. He crossed over to the mantelpiece, and, taking out his watch, wound the clock up. Then he heard something else.

With great care he laid the key softly on the mantelpiece and listened intently. The clock was now aggressively audible, so that he opened the case again, and putting his finger against the pendulum, stopped it. Then he drew his revolver and cocked it, and, with his set face turned towards the door, and his lips parted, waited.

At first—nothing. Then all the noises which a lonely man hears in a house at night. The stairs creaked, something moved in the walls. He crossed noiselessly to the door and opened it. At the head of the staircase he fancied the darkness moved.

"Who's there?" he cried in a strong voice.

Then he stepped back into the room and lit his lamp. "I'll get to bed," he said grimly; "I've got the horrors."

He left the gas burning, and with the lamp in his left hand and the pistol in his right slowly ascended the stairs. The first landing was clear. He opened the doors of each room, and, holding the lamp aloft, peered in. Then he mounted higher, and looked in the rooms, crammed from floor to ceiling with pledges, ticketed and placed on shelves. In one room he thought he saw something crouching in a corner. He entered boldly, and as he passed along one side of a row of shelves could have sworn that he heard a stealthy footfall on the other. He rushed back to the door, and hung listening over the shaky balusters. Nothing stirred, and, satisfied that he must have been mistaken, he gave up the search and went to his bedroom. He set the lamp down on the drawers, and turned to close the door, when he distinctly heard a noise in the shop below. He snatched up the lamp again and ran hastily downstairs, pausing halfway on the lowest flight as he saw a dark figure spreadeagled against the side door, standing on tiptoe to draw back the bolt.

At the noise of his approach, it turned its head hastily, and revealed the face of the brown man; the bolt shot back, and at the same moment the Jew raised his pistol and fired twice.

From beneath the little cloud of smoke, as it rose, he saw that the door stood open and that the figure had vanished. He ran hastily down to the door, and, with the pistol raised, stood listening, trying to peer through the fog.

An unearthly stillness followed the deafening noise of the shots. The fog poured in at the doorway as he stood there hoping that the noise had reached the ears of some chance passer-by. He stood so for a few minutes, and then, closing the door again, resolutely turned back and went upstairs.

His first proceeding upon entering his room was to carefully look beneath and behind the heavy, dusty pieces of furniture, and, satisfied that no foe lurked there, he closed the door and locked it Then he opened the window gently, and listened The court below was perfectly still. He closed the window, and, taking off his coat, barricaded the door with all the heaviest furniture in the room. With a feeling of perfect security, he complacently regarded his handiwork, and then, sitting on the edge of the bed, began to undress. He turned the lamp down a little, and reloading the empty chambers of his revolver, placed it by the side of the lamp on the drawers. Then, as he turned back the clothes, he fancied that something moved beneath them. As he paused, it dropped lightly from the other side of the bed to the floor.

At first he sat, with knitted brows, trying to see what it was. He had only had a glimpse of it, but he certainly had an idea that it was alive. A rat perhaps. He got off the bed again with an oath, and, taking the lamp in his hand, peered cautiously about the floor. Twice he walked round the room in this fashion. Then he stooped down, and, raising the dirty bed hangings, peered beneath.

He almost touched the wicked little head of the brown man's devil, and with a stifled cry, sprang hastily backward. The lamp shattered against the corner of the drawers, and, falling in a shower of broken glass and oil about his stockinged feet, left him in darkness. He threw the fragment of glass stand which remained in his hand from him, and, quick as thought, gained the bed again, and crouched there, breathing heavily.

He tried to think where he had put the matches, and remembered there were some on the widow-sill. The room was so dark that he could not see the foot of the bed, and in his fatuity he had barricaded himself in the room with the loathsome reptile which was to work the brown man's vengeance.

For some time he lay listening intently. Once or twice he fancied that he heard the rustle of the snake over the dingy carpet, and he wondered whether it would attempt to climb on to the bed. He stood up, and tried to get his revolver from the drawers. It was out of reach, and as the bed creaked beneath his weight, a faint hiss sounded from the floor, and he sat still again, hardly daring to breathe.

The cold rawness of the room chilled him. He cautiously drew the bed-clothes towards him, and rolled himself up in them, leaving only his head and arms exposed. In this position he began to feel more secure, until the thought struck him that the snake might be inside them. He fought against this idea, and tried to force his nerves into steadiness. Then his fears suggested that two might have been placed in the bed. At this his fears got the upper hand, and it seemed to him that something stirred in the clothes. He drew his body from them slowly and stealthily, and taking them in his arms, flung them violently to the other end of the room. On his hands and knees he now travelled over the bare bed, feeling. There was nothing there.

In this state of suspense and dread time seemed to stop. Several times he thought that the thing had got on the bed, and to stay there in suspense in the darkness was impossible. He felt it over again and again. At last, unable to endure it any longer, he resolved to obtain the matches, and stepped cautiously off the bed; but no sooner had his feet touched the floor than his courage forsook him, and he sprang hurriedly back to his refuge again.

After that, in a spirit of dogged fatalism, he sat still and waited. To his disordered mind it seemed that footsteps were moving about the house, but they had no terrors for him. To grapple with a man for life and death would be play; to kill him, joy unspeakable. He sat still, listening. He heard rats in the walls and a babel of jeering voices on the stair-case. The whole blackness of the room with the devilish, writhing thing on the floor became invested with supernatural significance. Then, dimly at first, and hardly comprehending the joy of it, he saw the window. A little later he saw the outlines of the things in the room. The night had passed and he was alive!

He raised his half-frozen body to its full height, and, expanding his chest, planted his feet firmly on the bed, stretching his long body to the utmost. He clenched his fist, and felt strong. The bed was unoccupied except by himself. He bent down and scrutinized the floor for his enemy, and set his teeth as he thought how he would tear it and mangle it. It was light enough, but first he would put on his boots. He leant over cautiously, and lifting one on to the bed, put it on. Then he bent down and took up the other, and, swift as lightning, something issued from it, and, coiling round his wrist, ran up the sleeve of his shirt.

With starting eyeballs the Jew held his breath, and, stiffened into stone, waited helplessly. The tightness round his arm relaxed as the snake drew the whole of its body under the sleeve and wound round his arm. He felt its head moving. It came wriggling across his chest, and with a mad cry, the wretched man clutched at the front of his shirt with both hands and strove to tear it off. He felt the snake in his hands, and for a moment hoped. Then the creature got its head free, and struck him smartly in the throat.

The Jew's hold relaxed, and the snake fell at his feet. He bent down and seized it, careless now that it bit his hand, and, with bloodshot eyes, dashed it repeatedly on the rail of the bed. Then he flung it to the floor, and, raising his heel, smashed its head to pulp.

His fury passed, he strove to think, but his brain was in a whirl. He had heard of sucking the wound, but one puncture was in his throat, and he laughed discordantly. He had heard that death had been prevented by drinking heavily of spirits. He would do that first, and then obtain medical assistance.

He ran to the door, and began to drag the furniture away. In his haste the revolver fell from the drawers to the floor. He looked at it steadily for a moment and then, taking it up, handled it wistfully. He began to think more clearly, although a numbing sensation was already stealing over him.

"Thirty thousand pounds!" he said slowly, and tapped his cheek lightly with the cold barrel.

Then he slipped it in his mouth, and, pulling the trigger, crashed heavily to the floor.

W.W. Jacobs – A Short Biography

William Wymark Jacobs was born on September 8, 1863 in the Wapping district of London, England. An author, humorist and dramatist, Jacobs is best remembered for the enduring classic tale of horror - "The Monkey's Paw".

As a youth, Jacobs grew up near the Wapping docks in London, where his father was a wharf manager. The family's first home was home was a house on a River Thames wharf.

The docklands setting would show up frequently in his later literary output. Jacobs, the wharf rat, and his three siblings lost their mother when they were all still young children. Their father, William Gage Jacobs, remarried and fathered a further seven children with his erstwhile housekeeper Ellen

Florey. Although he grew up surrounded by poverty, Jacobs himself received a formal education in London, first at a private prep school and later at the Birkbeck Literary and Scientific Institute (now part of the University of London and known as Birkbeck College).

Jacobs' adult working life began with a clerical position at the Post Office Savings Bank. The job was not a stimulating one but Jacobs put his imagination to good use and started to write short stories, sketches and articles, many of which appeared in the Post Office house publication "Blackfriars Magazine."

Although Jacobs did receive his fair share of rejection slips at the beginning of his career, many works written during this period of clerical employment appeared in the "Idler" and "Today" magazines, both of which were edited by noted humorist Jerome K. Jerome, who had taken a liking to Jacobs' stories.

From 1898, Jacobs also published stories in "The Strand", a popular, monthly fiction and general interest magazine. The arrangement stayed in place for most of his life and many of the works in Jacobs' subsequent collections – including the nautical serialization A Master of Craft (1899-1900) - appeared there first.

Jacobs' first volume of collected works was published in 1896. Many Cargoes, a selection of sea-faring yarns, established Jacobs as a popular writer and humorist with a penchant for authentic dialogue and trick endings (critics of the day referred to him as the "O. Henry of the Waterfront").

A year later he published a novelette, The Skipper's Wooing, and in 1898 and another collection of short stories titled Sea Urchins. These works painted vivid, if imaginatively stretched, pictures of dockland and seafaring London with colourful characters (such as "The Night Watchman", Ginger Dick) that now seem archetypal.

Many of Jacobs' periodical publications and first editions were illustrated with woodcuts and ink drawings, as was still the custom at the turn of the 20th century. The author worked regularly with artists such as E.W. Kemble, who had illustrated Mark Twain's Adventures of Huckleberry Finn and Harriet Beecher Stowe's Uncle Tom's Cabin, and his good friend Will Owen, who eventually became a household name on the strength of his iconic Bisto Kids, Bovril and Lux Soap advertising posters.

By 1899, Jacobs was able to quit the post office and finally begin a career making a living as a full-time writer.

He married the noted suffragist Agnes Eleanor Williams (who had been jailed for her protest activities) in 1900. They set up a household in Loughton, Essex as well as living part of the year in central London. The couple went on to have five children together though their marriage was considered an unhappy one.

The publication of two short novels: At Sunwich Port (a romantic tale of rival sea captains in the fictional seaside community of Sunwich standing in for the actual East England community of Sandwich, Kent) and Dialstone Lane (another small town romance involving intrigue and buried treasure), in 1902 and 1904 respectively, cemented Jacobs' reputation as one of the leading British authors of the new century.

On the foundations of a continuing ability to write for his audience he was readily published though he never strayed too far from what was becoming his familiar, dependable style. There followed a string of further successful publications, including Captain's All (1905), Night Watches (1914), The

Castaways (1916), and Sea Whispers (1926). Jacobs published eighteen books in all during his lifetime; thirteen collections and five novels.

As a storyteller, Jacobs is perhaps better remembered for a handful of brief tales of the supernatural than for his popular nautical-themed works. The most famous of these, The Monkey's Paw, originally appeared as part of the 1902 short story collection The Lady of the Barge. It is an economically written story about a shriveled talisman, a monkey's paw that brings grief and horror in the wake of all too literal wish granting. The story has been adapted for other media repeatedly, starting with a one-act play performed at London's Haymarket Theatre in 1903. There have been multiple film adaptations of the story in the modern era; some of us are familiar with its appearance in an episode of the popular animated series, The Simpsons.

Another macabre gem, The Toll-House, was published as part of the collection Sailor's Knots in 1909. Jacob's once again employs a sparse style to tell the story of a group of men who spend the night in a famously haunted house on a dare (a noticeably similar narrative concept was put to use in the much earlier play The Ghost of Jerry Bundler, which had launched Jacobs' parallel career as a dramatist back in 1899 when it was produced at the St. James Theatre in London). Innovative at the time of writing, these sparingly written, atmospheric ghost stories are now familiar classics of the supernatural genre.

Though prolific in his younger years, Jacobs' productivity dropped dramatically after the start of World War I. Yet even in self-imposed semi-retirement Jacobs was still recognized as a leading humorist, ranked alongside such writers as P. G. Wodehouse and George Birmingham. He enjoyed continuing influence and elevated status among his fellow writers as evidenced by these comments attributed to his colleague Henry James:

"Mr. Jacobs, I envy you. You are popular! Your admirable work is appreciated by a wide circle of readers; it has achieved popularity. Mine never goes into a second edition."

James' literary fortunes would, of course, change, but his back-handedly complimentary admiration is compelling evidence of Jacobs' reputation as a writer and humourist both for his audience and his perhaps more admired literary colleagues.

Though Jacobs would create little in the way of new work after 1911, he was still writing. In these later years, seemingly burnt out creatively, Jacobs concentrated more on writing dramatizations and adaptations of his existing stories, including Beauty and the Barge (a film version starring Margaret Rutherford was also released in 1937) and In the Dark (a one act play that is often performed pr published with The Monkey's Paw adaptation).

Though admired by loyal readers throughout his lifetime, Jacobs has been almost completely forgotten since. Critics are at a loss to name a single reason why - Jacobs is universally considered to be a fine and imaginative literary craftsman. But, as critic John Wain suggested in a 1960 essay, perhaps Jacobs' humour may have been too gentle to persist into the cruel and sarcastic modern era, his dry pokes at proletariat hardship no longer suiting the times.

Nonetheless, Jacobs' legacy remains solid: he continued Dickens' (a writer with whom he is also often compared) tradition for sharing working class stories in authentic vernacular. And polished narratives such as The Monkey's Paw set a standard for the clever use of horror in fiction and popular culture that endures to this day. Indeed recently his works have begun to show an increased demand and appreciation in a world that is constantly looking over its shoulder.

William Wymark Jacobs died in a North London nursing home in Hornsey Lane, Islington on September 1st, 1943, just a week before his 80th birthday.

W.W. Jacobs — A Concise Bibliography

NOVELS AND SHORT STORY COLLECTIONS
MANY CARGOES (SHORT STORIES) (1896)
THE SKIPPER'S WOOING (1897)
SEA URCHINS (SHORT STORIES) (1898) aka MORE CARGOES
A MASTER OF CRAFT (1900)
LIGHT FREIGHTS (SHORT STORIES) (1901)
THE LADY OF THE BARGE (SHORT STORIES) (1902)
AT SUNWICH PORT (1902)
DIALSTONE LANE (1902)
SALTHAVEN (1908)
CAPTAINS ALL (SHORT STORIES) (1911)
NIGHT WATCHERS (SHORT STORIES) (1914)
DEEP WATERS (SHORT STORIES) (1919)

SHORT STORIES (INCLUDING THOSE USED IN THE COLLECTIONS ABOVE)
A BENEFIT PERFORMANCE
A BLACK AFFAIR
A CASE OF DESERTION
A CHANGE OF TREATMENT
A CIRCULAR TOUR
A DISCIPLINARIAN
A DISTANT RELATIVE
A GARDEN PLOT
A GOLDEN VENTURE
A HARBOUR OF REFUGE
A LOVE KNOT
A LOVE PASSAGE
A MARKED MAN
A MIXED PROPOSAL
A RASH EXPERIMENT
A SAFETY MATCH
A SPIRIT OF AVARICE
A TIGER'S SKIN
ADMIRAL PETERS
AFTER THE INQUEST
ALF'S DREAM
AN ADULTERATION ACT
AN ELABORATE ELOPEMENT
AN INTERVENTION
AN ODD FREAK
ANGELS' VISITS
BACK TO BACK
BEDRIDDEN
THE WINTER OFFENSIVE

THE UNDERSTUDY
THE UNKNOWN
THE VIGIL
WATCH-DOGS
THE WEAKER VESSEL
THE WELL
THE WHITE CAT

STAGE
THE GHOST OF JERRY BUNDLER (1899) (In London)

FILM ADAPTATIONS
A MASTER OF CRAFT (1922)
THE MONKEY'S PAW (1933)
OUR RELATIONS, a Laurel & Hardy film, "suggested by" to Jacobs' "The Money Box." (1936)
FOOTSTEPS IN THE FOG, from the short story The Interruption. (1955)